A Sinner's Cry

By Rose Jackson-Beavers

Other Books by Rose Jackson-Beavers

❖ Backroom Confessions

❖ A Hole in My Heart

❖ Caught in the Net of Deceptions

❖ Sumthin' To Say

❖ Quilt Designs & Poetry Rhymes: A book of beautiful art pieces with poems about life & stuff

A Sinner's Cry

By Rose Jackson-Beavers

Published by Prioritybooks Publications
Florissant, Missouri

P. O. Box 2535

Florissant, MO 63033

Edited by: Lynel Johnson & Kendra Koger

Cover Designed by Sheldon Mitchell of Majaluk

Manufactured in the United States of America

Library of Congress Control Number: 2011916297

ISBN: 9780983486039

For information regarding discounts for bulk purchases, please contact Prioritybooks Publications at 1-314-306-2972 or rosbeav03@ yahoo. com.

Dedication

This book is dedicated to my parents L. J. and Connie Booker, my husband Cedric and my daughter Adeesha Beavers. Thank you all for allowing me to simply be me.

Acknowledgements

Thank you God for allowing me to do the things I love to do and for giving me the talents to write stories I enjoy reading. To all my fans, family, and friends who understand that no church, or church members are perfect, but perfection is reserved for the Almighty God. He is the only perfect person or spirit and when we have faith in Him, all things are possible. The Bible says in Matthew 7:7: Ask, and it shall be given you; seek, and ye shall find; knock, and it shall be opened unto you.

I am so glad God has afforded us with the opportunity to have those things which we want when we ask Him for it. To each of you who read, support and understand my stories I want to thank you with all my heart. Live your dreams to the fullest and always allow God to direct your path.

Special thanks to Lynel for making me understand that" patience is a virtue". I will be forever grateful to you for your honesty and support in pushing me to be the best writer possible. I am so glad that you are in my corner. Thank you Kendra for helping me to build my company and for being an integral part of my life, and my writing. Without your support and expertise in marketing and writing I wouldn't know what to do. But God in His infinite wisdom always put the right people in our lives during the most important time.

To my best friend Mary Stallworth, where would I be if I couldn't laugh at my life, stories and dreams with you? Thank you for listening and supporting me.

To Josephine Lewis, I love spending time with you for you are the one who inspire fabulous stories in my head. To

Brenda Hampton, you have been the best mentor ever and I know God will keep blessing you because you understand the true meaning, "To whom much is given, much is expected." Thank you for sharing yourself with me. To Toni and OOSA from day one you have been my supporter. Your honesty and acknowledgements have propelled me to be a better writer and a future force to be reckoned with. To my authors, especially Lydia, Brenda, Ann, Mary, Carletta, Stanley, Kareem and Keisha who always support me. Thank you. I wish all of you continue success as authors.

Edward Booker my writing partner, let's make 2012 the best. I appreciate you, brother, and say to you: always work at becoming a Christian, a better man, a great husband, father and then writer.

Finally to my siblings, Regina, Charlotte, Glorina, Chester and Johnaver, thanks for being in my life. You inspire me. Finally to my nieces and nephews, just work hard at always being the best, and remember with God, all things are possible.

To all of my readers, again, I sincerely thank you.

A Sinner's Cry

Exodus 20:14

Thou shalt not commit adultery

Chapter 1

Rinnnnnnng. Rinnnnng.

The sudden shrill of the phone jarred me awake. Pulling my hand from under the soft bed covers, I fumbled and patted the cherry wood nightstand in search of the sound that annoyed and interrupted my peaceful slumber. My fingers made contact with the hard receiver, as I lifted my head off my satin pillow and put it up to my ear. "Hello," I groaned as if in pain.

The woman on the other end screamed, "Who is this?!"

I rubbed the sleep from my eyes while I averted a yawn. "You called this number, so you should know." I closed my eyes and lay back down.

"This is Jill Tate, you trick."

My eyes popped open as if a fairy godmother had sprinkled dust in them. All the sleepiness I felt was gone. My body sprung up to attention as I turned on the lamp. The bright light temporarily blinded me. My heart began to pound like little staccato drums being brutally hit. I took a deep breath and released the irritation that threatened to consume me. Finally, I asked, after reeling my voice back into control, "Jill who?"

"Tate." The woman smacked her lips like she was sampling a sour piece of candy. "You know who I am. I'm tired of you little tricks sleeping with my husband."

"Sorry, but I think you have the wrong number," I said as I

rubbed my right eye.

"I don't think so. I checked my phone bill and your number is all over it. Your trifling ass is sleeping with my husband, Darren."

I sat straight up in bed and changed the phone from my left ear to the right one, trying to assure I heard what the woman had said. "Darren is not married, not the one I know."

"Are you serious? Is that it? Really, is that all it takes for a man to get into women's panties is to say he's not married?"

"Sorry, but the Darren I'm seeing is not married." My heart was beating hard inside my chest as my left hand balled up into a fist. I needed more information. I tried to think of what would be a good facial distinction to share with her to assure she had the wrong number and wrong man. "Is the Darren you're seeing a professor with green eyes?"

"You're not stupid. Yes, he has green eyes and I'm sure you knew he was married. All you skanks know. You're just playing a role like you don't."

Silence.

"The cat got your tongue, doesn't he, sucker? You can't say a word?" Jill's voice echoed so loud in my ear, I had to pull the phone away to prevent harm to my eardrum.

As I held the phone tightly, my right hand turned numb. I shook my hand, trying to get the blood moving again. I was getting angrier by the minute. Beads of sweat flowed down my oval-shaped face, colliding with the tears that stained my smooth mocha-colored skin. The phone call was real. The man I loved was not mine. He had a wife. I couldn't think nor swallow the saliva as it increased in my mouth. Activities we did together became blurred; the passion shared became foreign as I tried to remember how his hands had caressed my body. But what I felt at that moment was pain ingrained in my heart like rough sandpaper. How dare that snake make me believe I was the only one? Normally, I was quick on my feet with smart responses when faced with uncomfortable situations, but I couldn't think of anything substantial to say, so I blurted out, "You need to talk to him."

"I'm talking to you, trick, and I demand you stay away from him or your ass is grass. Leave my husband alone. He needs to be home with his wife and kids."

I hung up the phone and sat in the same spot frozen, unable to think about what to do next. As my nerves settled, I lifted my left hand to the side of my left temple and tried to wipe away the feeling of dread that crept over my skin like little ants roaming on an ant hill. I swiped away at the tingles that nagged my right arm.

Darren couldn't be married. I tried to reason by crossing out conversations as they rolled through my mind. Some of the conversations left more questions than answers. Why did he sometimes disappear when I needed him? Why did he sometimes rush me off the phone?

I grabbed the phone and punched his cell phone number into the phone pad. The phone rang until it went to voicemail. "Darren, please call me, it's urgent." I left message after message, as I lost hold of myself in my attempt to reach out to him. "Please call me back. Some woman called, Baby, and said you were her husband. Baby, please call me. I need to know if this is true." The calls were never returned. Darren always called back, so I was surprised he had not returned my voicemails. I began to feel the caller had told the truth. Lately, Darren had been slipping out of my bed. It seemed that he could not spend the night as he had done so many times before.

After I waited about two hours for him to call back, I lay down and cried until I fell asleep on my soaking wet, tear-stained pillow.

****

The next morning Darren arrived before nine A. M. I was headed to work. I was dressed in a red two-piece suit, but my 130-pound, well-toned body felt naked. To have someone call to say you are sleeping with their husband leaves you feeling unclean and vulnerable, like you need a bath. Every part of you is exposed. My heart pounded through my chest at a rapid pace. The doorbell rang and I darted to the door; I knew it was Darren. As I swung the door open with much force, the slight wind circulated the cologne I had given him. The scent wafted through the front door before he did. It assaulted my nostrils and floated through them with a fierceness that made my knees buckle. Oh, how good this man smelled and how good he looked in his dark Armani suit that fitted his body as if the seamstress had made it just for him.

"Baby, I got all your messages. Let me explain." He

reached his arms out to me as if my five-foot-three stature would just fall into them. I stepped back.

"Are you married?" I asked in a pitiful, wounded voice. Tears welled up in the corners of my eyes, threatening to cascade like a river down my face.

"Yes, but we filed for divorce. It's over with us. It's been over a longtime." He looked down like a rat caught in a trap as he begged to be released from the contraption causing him pain. His eyes looked puffy like he had either been hit in them or as if he had not slept in days.

Slap! The sound across his face exploded like a huge wave slamming against hard steel. He tried to grab my hands to stop the sudden thrashing against his body. My hands and arms flapped out of control as they swung at him in all directions. The hits jabbed and punched him in every part of his face and chest. My mocha-colored fists began to blur as they pounded into his ribcage. He grabbed my hands to slow the rhythmic thuds that battered his chest and stomach. With the right eye-hand coordination, he was able to secure my arms stiff against his body with a firm grip. "Stop it, Denise. Stop it now."

"Let me go!" I cried out between sobs as I tried to wiggle out of his embrace. "You are hurting me." He loosened his grip and I dropped to the floor in agony. Nothing could have hurt more. "Get out, Darren. Just get out."

"You don't mean that. I love you."

As I looked up at him, the frown on my face thickened at the nonsense this man had spilled out of his mouth. "Love?

5

What do you know about love, you cheating dog? I trusted you!"

Darren's eyes widened as he bent down to my level and grabbed my hands. If he had not been holding me so tight, I would have attacked him again. He blinked back tears. "You don't mean that. I can explain everything. Just listen to me."

"Get out!" I screamed. "I said get out of my house!" Hurt by his deceit, my voice roared like thunder. The rumble snapped him out of his trance-like stance. Not wanting to upset me anymore than I was; he stood up, turned around on the shiny wooden floors and walked briskly to the door. As he neared the doorway, he turned back. Looking over his shoulders with his beady swollen eyes, he said, "This isn't over."

As he walked out, he slammed the door behind him. I sat on the foyer floor for about ten minutes. I bawled until the heat that beamed off the window warmed my skin. The sun's hot rays were dangerous to my unprotected skin, but I couldn't move. It caused the suit I wore to stick to my clammy, sweat-soaked body. Embarrassed by the snot that bubbled out every time I took another deep breath and let out another sob, I forced myself to get up. To do so, I had to crawl toward the hall's table and use it like an anchor to pull up my weakened and angry body. This was the second Friday in March, my favorite month. Instead of laughter, excitement and happiness, as I planned my wardrobe for tonight's activity with some friends, I felt like someone had knocked my teeth out of my mouth. Instead of preparation for a lovers' weekend, I felt sad and broken. My heart felt like someone had taken a hammer and cracked it into little pieces. How could I celebrate love when the love I had was not real?

After I pulled up on the table, I walked to the living room like a dead man taking his final walk right before being electrocuted. I grabbed the phone when I reached my destination. I gathered all my emotions, put them in check and breathed in hard as I prepared to talk calmly to my secretary. When the secretary answered the phone I told her I would not be in and then called my mother. Standing there, listening to the phone ring, I breathed in hard to control the sad, squeaky voice laced with pain that had become routine when I was upset. When I heard my mother pick up the phone I said, "Hello."

"Denise, is this you?" my mother asked in a soothing voice, reflective of soft jazz.

The words lingered in my throat.

"Denise. Honey, what's wrong?"

I felt like a little child who needed the comfort of her parent. At the sound of Mother's voice, I gathered strength and whispered with a childlike soft voice, "Mommy, I need you."

****

Before leaving to visit Mother, I showered again to knock the sweat off. As the water battered me in all the right places, I grabbed the soap and let the sweet smell of strawberries soothe me. I dried off, oiled my body down with Shea butter and put on a pair of blue jeans and a T-shirt. Brushing my sweaty, long, brownish-black, damp hair into a ponytail, I dabbed some brandy-colored lipstick on to mask how drained and broken I looked. I grabbed my purse, searched for the car keys, located them on the table in the foyer, put on a light jacket to ward off the thin chill in the air, set the house alarm and left. I drove thirty-five minutes to mother's house.

As I drove to Mom's, it occurred to me that Darren had provided so many signs of another woman being in his life. There were times he would leave early, arrive at my house at awkward unscheduled times, not answer his phone after he checked to see who was calling and the big one, going into the bathroom while lifting his finger to his mouth to shush me as he shut the door before talking on the phone. He would later explain it was the Dean of Students or the president of the college. Like a fool, I believed him because I didn't want to think he was seeing anyone else. I took the reasonable route and put my wild imagination into the back of my mind where I allowed it to stay under lock and key.

As I drove down the highway with plenty of time to cry again, I dried the tears that ran down my face with the back of my hand. Every now and then I banged my open hand against the steering wheel to punish myself for getting caught up, which was something I promised myself I would never do. One thing was certain: If I lived through this pain, I could make it through anything.

Chapter 2

As I drove, I had plenty of time to think. I wondered if my secretary heard the pain in my voice when I called her earlier to let her know I would not be coming into the office. After I pulled into the driveway, I opened the car door, grabbed a baby wipe out of the package laying on my car seat and then wiped my tear-stained eyes. Then I opened the car door and got out. I prayed, "*Lord, please help me to soothe the pain in my heart.*"

It was so easy to talk to Mother now; unlike it was when I was a teenager. It's been said that when you are a baby up to about twelve years old, you need your parents for survival. You can't survive without your mom. As you become a teenager, from about thirteen until around the age of eighteen, your mom is considered old-fashioned, and doesn't know anything about life; getting on your nerves with her outdated information. Then when you become a card-holding, full-fledged adult, you can't live without your mom because now you are best friends. You go back to respecting and needing your mom just like you did when you were a child.

That's where I was, needing Mom because I was lower than low with a heart that seemed broken into a million pieces. I needed Mother to help put my heart back together again.

Using the key to open the door, I walked into the living room and plopped down on the couch. The couch seemed to bounce up to reach out and hug me. When I relaxed my back into the plush white Oriental couch, it sunk in as if it was conforming to my body. It felt good being home. When Mom walked into the living room, her footsteps sounded like a little ball being bounced in a slow pace. As she dried her hands with a terrycloth towel and took off her powder blue apron, she asked, "What's wrong, Sweetheart?" Before I reacted, I closed my eyes and inhaled the scent of the sweet-smelling potato pie that reeked of cinnamon and nutmeg. Alas, I was home with the person who loved me enough to cook my favorite dessert and help me through a difficult time. I tilted my head up to assure the scent would float into my nose and somehow attack my taste buds.

My mother parked her medium-sized body right next to me. It seemed she wanted her daughter to feel the closeness of her body and to remember she could always come to her no matter what.

This is gonna be hard. I cleared my throat and tried to sandbag the water that was about to leak out of my eyes, but it didn't work. The tears splashed down like a river. Mom reached over and hugged me. As she patted my back, she whispered, "When you're ready to talk, I'm here."

We stayed in that position for about five minutes. Mom just hugged me tight while she allowed the tears to fall and wash away all the hurt and pain. After I composed myself, I sat up to straighten out my back, wiped my tears using the bottom of my T-shirt and then turned to look at Mom. "Mom," I mumbled as if talking loud would do me more harm, "Darren is married. He lied to me."

Reaching her hand out to stroke my cheek, she said, "I'm so sorry to hear that, Honey. I'm just so sorry."

"His wife called me." I rubbed my hands together, trying to eliminate my nervousness. Mom looked at me with raised eyebrows, but she didn't say anything.

I leaned forward and rested my forearms on my leg. As more tears fell, I reached up and wiped my eyes again. "I never suspected it. I trusted him and believed that we had something special."

Mom wrapped her arms around my shoulders to comfort me. "It's amazing how the truth always finds a way to come out. I'm sorry you have to go through this. Only input I can offer you is that it will get better. I know that doesn't mean much to you now while you are in pain, but with prayer, you will become stronger."

Taking a deep breath, I reared back into the comfort of the couch and retorted, "I know Mom; it just hurts when someone breaks your heart."

"I understand." Again she looked at me like she wanted to say something, but I could tell she didn't want to hurt me any further. With her eyebrows arched up and thick lines laced across her forehead, she said again, "I'm so sorry you are going through this."

As we sat there talking about Darren and his wife, I found Mom to be witty and smart. She made me laugh so many times; talking about how Darren would get what was coming to him. "Karma is something, you know?" She even said, "I betcha his wife kicked his tail." I laughed as I thought about his puffy fat eyes. While we talked, Mom convinced me to go to church with her the next day; I said I would. As we chatted, Mom reached over to hug me again. It felt so comforting.

"Mom, I haven't been to church in some time now."

"I know, but I didn't understand why? I know you tried to explain, but you know me."

I rubbed the right side of my temple, a habit I tried to get rid of, but still lacked the fortitude to do. "I couldn't find an Adventist church close enough in college. Once I came back to St. Louis and settled in, I just stopped going."

"You know I have tried to get you to return to church ever since you came back home. I knew you were not attending, but I didn't know why. But one thing is sure; when you are raised in church, rarely will you stay away."

As we finished talking, I assured her I would see her the next day, but first, I had to have a piece of that sweet-smelling, sweet potato pie whose scent continued to linger throughout the house.

****

Bright and early Saturday morning I pulled onto the parking lot peppered with small rocks and turned the car off. I reared back into the leather car seat to relax for one minute. I sat there and watched and admired the people going into The True Church. As I gawked at the people arriving, they twisted and twirled in their best Sabbath clothes while they treaded to the front of the big brick ranch-style church to worship their God. The women were dressed in large pastel-colored hats that matched their outfits. The men walked around with their arms outstretched to the waiting arms of women who basked in being hugged by the brothers of the church. Some women got out of their cars and glided into the parking lot with smiles pasted across their faces, ready to brighten up someone's life as their faces beamed with happiness. Some reached out their manicured hands to shake the hands of others. With stress-free smiles that seemed to burst with sunlight, they looked happy to see each other. As more cars pulled up onto the parking lot, more passengers jumped out and briskly walked into the church's big wooden front double doors like they knew a secret that they were coming to find out about.

While I sat there I thought about something Mother once said years ago. I remembered that conversation as if it occurred minutes before. Mother walked into the country-style kitchen, decorated in white and blue wallpaper. She did her best to push me to get ready for church by speaking loud and fast, "Get ready Denise, I do not want to be late." I was moving slow, still needing to put on my shoes. It wasn't that I didn't want to go to church, but I felt that people were fake, who only showed their concern at church while jumping up, shouting and spinning around as if they had spent their entire week feeding and serving the poor when in fact they had done nothing, but party, drink and dance to the heavy musical beats of whatever musical artist was popular at that moment.

I just did not want to partake in the fakery, and didn't feel like dressing up in some cutesy clothing and hot stockings to go join the dog and pony show of women and men who had probably spent several hours during the week sinning. The same people who rushed to be the first ones to sit on the front pew of the church as if they did nothing but praise God and read their Bibles while fasting and praying daily. That day I started the conversation with mother. It was best to beat her to the punch anyway.

"Mother, I'm sorry. Today is a beautiful Saturday

morning and I'm not feeling church, so I'm not going."

"Who do you think you are? This is the Sabbath! You know we go to church today. You're not grown, so you do what I say and I say get ready now!" Mom had that look on her face where the lines raced across her forehead signifying she was getting upset; she was about to slaughter her child.

"Mother, I am grown. I'm a high school graduate and I'm eighteen."

"That's not grown. Grown is living in your own home and paying your way through life. Until you can do that without using your parents' resources, you are not grown, you're just smelling yourself."

"I can't wait to get out of here." I walked away in search of my black sandals.

"I can't wait until you get out either, and since you're still here, be ready in ten minutes. I mean it."

I walked away stomping like the child Mother had just called me. See, the problem was I knew that some of the women I'd seen in the church were not real Christians. On Friday night they were in the same clubs I went to and I had danced right next to some of them; I kind of felt like they were fake. Then, when their lives were in a major uproar with problems, they would track to church, seeking God to solve them. It was like they did their dirt in the city and headed to the altar for help when they became burdened. That didn't set well with me.

At mother's insistence, I got ready and jumped in the car

with Mrs. Betty Reese. *"Mom, why are you making me go to church when you know that many of those folks aren't true Christians?"*

As she drove to church I noticed the lines across Mom's forehead. She called them angry lines and at that point I knew I had pushed her buttons. She turned the corner so fast that had the car door been open, I would have been laid out on the hot pavement. Then she hit a bump that sent us both toward the ceiling of her car.

"Sorry about that. But you know how I feel about talking negative about people. I didn't raise you like that. I expect more. I've told you more times than I have fingers and toes that the church is like a hospital; people go there to get better. If they were perfect they wouldn't need God. I expect to see problems because we are all trying to grow in the Lord. Do you understand?"

"I understand, but some of the members are wild."

"Well, I don't care to hear anything negative. Talk to me when you want to help the situation."

That was it. Mother had the last word. That was how I felt about people and their running to church for help when they were in trouble and today, seven years later, I still feel the same way.

Chapter 3

As I sat in the parking lot, people-watching, my mood shifted from feeling anxious to moody. At first I was nervous about going to church to see old friends and to get "a healing" as the old folks called it. My heart raced and my hands were sweaty. I couldn't stop tapping the steering wheel. No matter how hard I tried to get Darren out of my system by dwelling on the negative things about him, my heart held on. I thought about the time he farted and I fled the room. Or the time he had a piece of the greens I'd cooked stuck in his front tooth. I even thought about his stinking, big feet. Yet those memories couldn't overshadow what I felt in my heart. As I sat in my black Lexus, with my head reared back and eyes closed, I reminisced about the first time we met.

"Hello."

I looked up from the business book I was studying, breathed in hard to demonstrate the frustration I felt from the intrusion that interrupted my studies. *"Hi,"* I said as I bent my head back down and continued to read.

"Are you a business major?" He pulled the chair out and sat down at the table without asking.

"Yes," I answered, but didn't look up, which should have showed him that I was not satisfied with him invading my space.

"My name is Darren."

With clenched teeth, I said, *"Denise."*

"Nice meeting you, Denise."

As I looked up to scold him, to tell him to move, I saw the most beautiful light-green eyes staring back. I breathed in to control the energy rising between my thighs. Since that day, we'd been inseparable, attending all kinds of off-campus activities like movies, baseball and football games; we even went dancing. Now, I felt so dumb. For goodness sake, I was the manager of a huge social services department, but couldn't even determine if one person was playing me for a fool.

****

As I sat there and thought about who I was and tried to figure out why this happened to me, I imagined myself at a broken women's meeting, a place for women to go to who were tricked into dating married men. Although I didn't think one existed, if one did, I would say:

I am a fool. My name is Denise Maria Reese and I am twenty-five years old. I am searching for something to make me feel whole. Sometimes I feel like a part of me is missing. Like others, I put on a happy face, but inside I am dying. I am dying because my heart is broken. I just found out that my long-term boyfriend was already married. I tried hard to leave him, but my heart is holding on like roots in an old tree.

I'm from a small family, have one younger sister, Terri, who just turned twenty and a brother, Don, who is seventeen. I get along with most people because of my carefree style. I graduated from a college near Chicago and received my bachelor's and master's degrees in Social Work, Sociology and Business Administration. I work at a local organization as a high-level manager and I have been with the Department of Social Services for four years. I own my own home and financially, I'm doing quite well. Unfortunately, even though I make six figures, have invested well and have an amazing financial portfolio, I am not married and was searching for love. What I found was a lie, a big old rusty, handsome liar.

I was raised in church and spent most of my life holding some kind of church office. I was baptized at fourteen, but I will admit that I did it because my mother was being re-baptized into a new faith. We were Baptists until my mother was invited to a different church by her friend. Once she visited and took Bible classes, she realized that we were not keeping the right day as the Sabbath. In a matter of months, we left our Baptist church home, friends and relatives and joined the Shiloh Seventh Day Adventist Church, better known as the True Church, where we attend church on Saturdays.

I called my mother because she always makes me feel better by giving me the love and attention I need. Mom would caress my face and say, "God will make a way." To soothe my aching heart she asked that I attend church with her.

Deuteronomy 20:1 states: "Remember the Sabbath and keep it holy." After keeping nothing holy, I decided to go to church. I had spent the night before dancing at a club with some friends who had decided to join me in my pity party after I called to tell them I needed them. There I sat in a parking lot, staring at people who needed Jesus, just like I needed Him.

19

As a social service administrator, I knew that if I really was at a meeting I would never share that much information about my life, but it helped to feel better about being duped.

The more I thought about church, the more I realized I was doing what most people did. They leave church when their lives are going well and return when they are down and out and need to be uplifted. I was a sinner. My soul was hurt and my heart broken. As I stared at the people on the church grounds, I saw one young lady I recognized from Club Spotlight last night. Then I remembered what Mother had told me about church being the hospital for those needing Jesus.

As I stepped out of the car, Sister Clarice Clay approached. I recalled from years ago Sister Clay was a gossiper and troublemaker. I once heard her in the bathroom blasting out many of the women in the congregation, even talking about a visitor's worn clothing. She was talking to another member, but was loud enough for Sister Denison, the visitor, to hear her. I was a little peeved at Sister Clay and the woman she was speaking to, because they should have exhibited kinder feelings and pleasantries to the visitor and made her feel welcomed. Instead of helping her, they harmed her self-esteem. Eventually, I walked up to the lady, introduced myself and took her to my mother who was serving as a hostess. I was young, but those older women who should have known better, were acting ignorant and starting trouble.

Sister Clay was a beautiful lady, who wore a long weave that was detectable. If I tried to tell her about it, I'm pretty sure she would have knocked me out with harsh words.

"Aren't you Betty Reese's daughter?"

"Yes," I replied as I reached out to shake her hand. "I am."

"Good to see you, child. Where have you been? The last I heard you were no longer in the church. Doing well financially, I heard. Got a good job, don't you? Look at this car, what is it? A Mercedes or is it one of those expensive Lexus cars?"

Hoping the lady would slow her roll and stop asking rapid fire questions, I just looked at her. Not responding to those questions, I murmured, "It's nice seeing you." I turned to walk away, but Sister Clay ran up and kept right on with her probing.

"Are you married, Denise?"

"No, I'm not. You are Ms. Clay, right?"

"Yes, darling. What brings you back to our neck of the woods? I heard you had a nice house out in St. Louis somewhere. Got any babies?"

I couldn't believe it. The woman was talking so fast, her lips opened and closed like a blinking exit sign. "No! I don't, but it was nice talking to you. I'll have to talk to you later."

I pivoted around and walked away. As a matter of fact, I took off jogging to get away from her. She was still the same person. I thought about people in church; some of them were there to cause problems. If what Mom said was true about churches being like hospitals, when would some of the folk ever get better? After all, you can't stay in the hospital forever with the same illness. Some of those people should have been healed and released by now.

I walked into the sanctuary and sat next to my mother and sister who were sitting in the fifth pew from the front of the church. I was tired from dancing at the club the night before and had spent some time talking to Darren on the phone when I returned home. He asked me for another chance at being together. He promised he did love me and that things would work out. But I was still angry. Even though I'd considered seeing him again, I knew it was wrong. It was going to be difficult to break up with him because my heart was entrenched into him like vines growing on the side of a brick house. I yawned and covered my mouth as I thought about how I was like other people who ran to God when all else failed. Even though I hated that folk only sought God for problems, it was my turn to do the same thing.

Pastor James Davis was new to me. He was a tall, peanut-colored handsome man. He had deep dimples and a perfectly round head. His eyes were bright and he had the whitest teeth and longest eyelashes I'd seen on a man. He wore his hair in a low fade. I could see his arm muscles bulging out of his two-piece preaching suit. The fitness center must have been his best friend.

As I examined him, I could tell the women in the church were impressed with him. With every word he said, sisters hollered, "Amen!" Sometimes, even before he finished his statement. The sermon he preached was called, "Breaking Down the Walls of Jericho." He was animated. As he walked from behind the pulpit, he clasped his hands together. "You need to break down the walls of Jericho. How are you going to break down the walls to your problems when Jesus is not the center of your life? To make Jesus your center, the most important person in your life, you are going to have to give up drinking, give up smoking, using drugs, and having sexual relationships with people you are not married to. You are going to have to break down the walls."

"Amen," screamed Ms. Clay as she rose to her feet. Soon women were standing up and some had started shouting. Brother Johnson shouted, "Pastor, you gon' have to listen to your own words!"

"Woo hoo!" Brother Johnson shouted. As he swiveled around the pew, he laughed. "All these hypocrites up in this church are acting like they're so perfect."

The whole church ignored him. I observed him as he watched and waited for another opportunity to hurl insults toward the pastor and the congregation. No longer sleepy, I turned to Mother, and whispered, "Who is that man?"

"We'll talk at home." She returned her attention to the pastor.

When I looked up, the elders of the church were putting fake bricks all around the pastor, like they were building a wall around him. The pastor sweated and swung his arms like he was pushing things out of his way, the whole church was up on their feet, and even I was excited.

"Faith broke down the walls and you are going to have to do the same thing, too. You can't sit back and keep wondering why you are having so many problems while God is not the center of your life. You gon' have to give it all up, you must give up the running in the streets all night, give up the cheating and lying and stealing. Put away the negative comments about your neighbors and stop holding others back with your gossip and innuendoes. Church, if you want God to bless you, you need to knock the walls down, kick them and break through them."

As he pushed himself through the fake wall, the church folks were up on their feet, clapping. Folk were crying and waving their handkerchiefs in the air. Ushers rushed to the side of maybe four members who were up on their feet, dancing, crying and screaming, "Jesus! Jesus! Oh, yes, Jesus!" The Holy Spirit hit me and I stood up too. The momentum in the church was at an all-time high. Not one person was sitting down. Tears were running down my face. It felt as if he was talking to me. I had lain with another woman's husband. Even though I found out after dating him, I was already in too deep. My feelings were involved and when that happens, most women just stay. Men are smart like that. They know that if they can keep seeing you long enough to make you care about them, they got you for the long haul. Once your feelings get involved with a married man you turn a blind eye to his family. If you can have a little part of him, then you're okay. For me though, I promised myself that I would never mess around with a married man. Nothing could make me break someone else's sacred vows; that was until Darren. He was the kind of man who made women salivate and become sexually excited just from looking at him.

Because of how I was raised, I didn't know anyone who dated married men. I only knew people who were in long-term relationships. My parents were married for thirty years and during that time many women tried to get to Dad, but as far as Mom knew, he stayed faithful to her and our family.

I learned so much about men as an adult. If a man could get away with messing around, he would. Most men want their cake and the ice cream too. If they could get a little on the side, why not? They'd stay with the other women as long as they allow them to see them outside of their marriage. Most of the time, women who date married men just let them soothe over their feelings, jump into their panties and when they are through with them, they go right back to their wives.

Sadly, what most women don't realize is that statisticians report that more than eighty percent of the men who have extramarital affairs never leave their wives. With stats like that, why do we women keep getting involved with men who are not solely involved with us?

The sermon was so powerful it made me feel as if I could move forward as long as I stayed close to God. To do that I knew I needed to stay in church. I planned to do just that.

∗∗∗∗∗∗∗∗∗∗∗∗∗

After the service was over, I walked through the receiving line to shake the pastor's hand. While in line, I noticed that Sister Clay was standing in the corner, staring in my direction. Her face was all scrunched up with wrinkles everywhere and her lips were curled up to her nose. She looked funny, like she could smell a skunk nearby.

As I shook the pastor's hand, I smiled. "Hi, Pastor, that was a wonderful, powerful service." I ignored Sister Clay.

"Thank you. Who are you?" He wiped the sweat off his forehead with a handkerchief.

"I'm Sister Betty Reese's daughter, Denise."

"Yes, you are. You look just like your mother. She speaks highly of you."

With a wide sparkling smile pasted on my face, I responded, "Thank you, Pastor."

Holding my hand firmly, he replied, "You'll visit with us again?"

"Yes I will." I released his hand and moved through the line, looking straight ahead.

Sister Clay grabbed my hand and pulled me roughly through the sea of folk still chatting in the vestibule. "Hey Denise, I want you to meet someone. Denise Reese, this is Teresa Berry."

Both of us stopped abruptly. "Hi, Teresa."

"Denise, I told Teresa about your success. Aren't you a doctor or something?

I know you are supposed to be in the medical field."

"No, I'm not a doctor. I'm in the social services field."

"Well, you must be high up in management because I heard you make a lot of money."

The conversation was uncomfortable. Ms. Nosy was getting on my nerves. We'd just met again after seven years, less than two hours ago. I was bothered by her actions. Church was supposed to be a place of peace, where I could go and forget about my problems, therefore, I refused to allow Ms. Clay to mess with my spirit.

After I said goodbye, I turned to walk away, but Sister Clay pulled me back around. "Would you like to go to my house for dinner? You and Teresa are invited."

"Maybe next time, I'm going to my mother's, but thank you."

With feet planted like stones on the ground, I made a U-turn so fast that I left black heel marks on the shiny floor. I had to get out of that church and away from that woman no matter how much of my heel I'd lost.

I couldn't believe Sister Clay had acted like we were friends. She must have been at least twenty-five years older than me. I didn't even know her that well and didn't want to. She was a gossiper and a busybody. I had to be careful not to say too much around her or I'd find myself in another mess. I tried to stay away from trouble; not run to it.

"Where is my mother?" I whispered. *I know she didn't leave me.* As I walked out the front door of the church, a hand touched my shoulder. It was the pastor.

Turning to face him, I smiled. "Hi again, Pastor, I enjoyed your sermon. It hit home."

His smile was beautiful. He had perfect kissing lips. I giggled at the way they curled when he smiled. "I'm glad you enjoyed it and more than anything I am happy you worshipped with us. Will you come again?" He reached out to take my hand into his.

I looked down at his hand, which had mine cupped inside of his. "Yes, I'll be back."

"Well, I look forward to seeing you again." He held my hand, not wanting to release it.

As I walked away, I wondered why the pastor was smiling like a Cheshire cat. *Isn't he taken or something? I heard he's single, but I don't know, you hear so much. That's definitely a question for Mom.*

Mother was in the parking lot, laughing all up in some brother's face. She was acting as if she had a crush on the man she was talking to. I stood by the car and watched the people as they laughed and talked to each other. They all seemed so happy and so excited to be in each other's presence. People seemed to enjoy each other. There were a lot of hugs being given out and plenty of laughter to spread around. It felt a little like a class reunion with folks jumping up and down excitedly talking to each other. They discussed their families, jobs and what they had planned to cook and eat after church. Some sisters were spinning around in their Sabbath best, modeling their outfits as if they were on a runway.

I watched in amazement. "Hi, Sister," someone said. Another brother shook my hand, "Welcome and please come again."

"Thanks. I will."

"Aren't you Denise Reese?"

"Yes, I am."

"I'm Sister Jones, Karen's mom," another member said.

"Oh, it's so nice to see you. How are you and how's Karen?"

"Karen is in the military. Just had a baby, and as a matter of fact, I spoke to her the other day and she asked about you."

"You don't say. What did she have?"

"A daughter, her first child and my first grandchild."

"That's wonderful. Tell her congratulations and when she comes to town look me up. We used to be great friends. We lost touch when we left for college."

"Well, it's good to see you again. Please visit with us again. If you need anything, we still have the same phone number. I'll be sure to let her know that we talked."

"Thank you so much and take care." I reached out to hug her.

Now that was a nice visit. Sister Jones was always such a nice person and active in Karen's life. She used to drop us off at school activities and at the skating rink. She was always mentoring and helping the youth in church. She was a good Christian woman. It was so good seeing her.

I was ready to leave, so I walked over to mother and interrupted her conversation with the nice-looking man. "I'm on my way to your house."

"All right, baby. This is Mr. Slaughter. You don't know him. He's a new member. Mr. Slaughter, this is my daughter, Denise."

I extended my hand to shake his. "Nice meeting you."

He gripped my hand and shook it. "You, too."

I turned to jog to the car because I didn't want anyone else to say anything to me. I entered the car, and then drove out of the parking lot to my mother's house. Mother had spent Friday cooking dressing, turkey, macaroni and cheese, turnip greens, cakes and sweet potato pies. She was a great cook. I had hoped we could spend some time together, but that wouldn't happen because she said that she had invited her best friend, Sarah, and two of the head church elders over for dinner. After church, everybody always invited each other to their homes for dinner. Everyone tried to complete their cooking before Friday's sundown. Since Seventh Day Adventists kept the Sabbath holy from sundown Friday night to sundown Saturday night, no cooking or cleaning was done during that time.

As we sat at the table, enjoying good conversation and eating a meal fit for a king, the doorbell rang. I patted my mouth with my napkin, laid it down on the table in front of me, and then stood up to go answer the door. I looked out of the peephole and was shocked to see Sister Clay.

Chapter 4

My head started hurting immediately. My first reaction was to ignore the doorbell and head back to the table to finish my meal in peace, but I knew mother would be upset if I disrespected her church member. So I opened the door with great reservation and stood there blocking the entrance to the hallway.

Sister Clay had this look of determination on her face, like she didn't care what anybody said, she was coming into Betty Reese's house. I was persistent that she was not about to come and hound me by questioning what I did and whom I did it with.

Standing on her toes and peeping over my shoulder, Sister Clay said, "Hi, Denise, is your mom here? I saw her car and Elder Bryant's and Elder Grant's cars."

Sister Clay almost knocked me down as she pushed past me to get into the dining room area. "Excuse me, Sister Clay, but you almost knocked me over." By now I was grinding my back teeth together, which was something I did when I was beyond pissed off. I also rubbed the side of my temple.

"Oh, sorry, baby, I didn't mean to push you. I smelled that great food and had to get to it. You know your mom is one of the best cooks at the church."

"Come into the dining room. Are you staying to eat?"

Strutting through the hallway like she owned it, she indicated, "You didn't think I drove all the way here to look at you all eating, did you?"

Ooooh, I do not like this woman. "Follow me to the ladies' room to wash your hands."

She popped her finger in the air. "Sure, honey, I'm following the leader."

I led her to the bathroom, and then went back to the kitchen and pulled out a plate. I picked up a glass goblet and silverware and placed her setting down near Mother because I wasn't about to spend time chatting with someone I didn't like.

Sister Clay returned to the table. She picked up her plate and checked it for spots. *I know that heifer didn't do that.* She asked Elder Grant to pass her the dressing. She continued asking everyone to pass her this and that until she had enough food on her plate to fill up a bear. If eyes could cut, mine would have split her in half. As she stuffed her big mouth with food and started talking with a mouth full of turkey, she said through her smacking, "You know, Denise, I saw the way the pastor was staring at you. I think he has a little crush on you."

Mother interjected, "Sister Clay, we won't be starting any rumors about the pastor at my table."

Great shot, Momma. Momma made me proud. But you know how gossipers are, it would take much more than what Mom had thrown at her to stop her from probing.

"Oh, honey, it's not a rumor. I saw Pastor stare and stutter the moment Denise walked in. After all, she is a gorgeous girl with a beautiful shape. Made the pastor forget what he was talking about. So you gon' go out with him?" She smiled as she stuffed a piece of turkey into her mouth.

Why is this hillbilly, polka dot and stripes wearing intruder here? I'ma slap that juice dripping from her big mouth into the front yard.

Elder Grant grunted, grabbed his napkin and dabbed the corners of his mouth. "Now, Sister Clay, you know that ain't right for you to come to this table with that mess. I'm sorry, but I am gonna call it like it is. You starting rumors and God don't like that stuff."

Elder Grant was a nice man. Our family had known him since I was a little kid. He stood by our family during so many moments of pain and despair. He was a six-foot-five, dark-skinned man with bulky shoulders. He weighed about 250 pounds, but he carried it well. He was not married. More than ten years had passed since his fiancée had left him at the altar and ran off with a deacon from another church, yet he was not bitter. He felt that at forty-eight, he had plenty of time for God to lead him to a wife whom he could love and cherish. He was dating a nice woman who was new to the church. She was out of town, visiting her ill mother.

Elder Grant never bit his tongue. He said just what he felt—straight, clear and to the point. Most people couldn't handle that, but he had plenty of admirers and friends who loved him, including our family.

"Elder Grant, now you know I didn't mean anything by what I said. You have two educated, single, good-looking people who would make a good couple. I just think Denise should check the pastor out, that's all." Sister Clay put a fork full of dressing in her mouth.

"Don't worry," I exclaimed. "You don't have to worry about me and the pastor getting together, I have a man." *Oh no, I didn't mean to say that.* "Sorry."

"It's no one's business anyway, and there's nothing to be ashamed about. This conversation is over. Cake, anyone?" Mom, the quick thinker, said as she passed the cake platter around the table.

The troublemaker was the first to say, "I want a piece of the German chocolate cake and a slice of sweet potato pie."

"Are you ladies planning on attending the church business meeting next Sabbath evening?" asked Elder Bryant who had been quiet most of the dinner. He turned to face Mom who stated that she planned to attend. I remained quiet.

Elder Bryant went on to explain the importance of the meeting. He said that it would be a business meeting to discuss church repairs. As he talked, I looked at Sister Clay; she had the funniest look on her face. "You know," she said, "I believe that someone is taking the money we have saved as a church to make regular repairs. All the pastor is going to do is beg for more money from the members. I just think that is wrong to keep asking us for money."

"Sister Clay, if the members of the church don't keep up the repairs, who do you think should?"

Ms. Clay said, "Elder Bryant, I'm just saying that we shouldn't have to keep giving our money. That's just plain wrong to me."

"I'm so sorry that you feel that way. If most of the members felt like you do, we would not be able to keep the doors of the church open."

"I second that," Mom said.

As I sat there, staring at Sister Clay, I wondered what could have happened in her life to make her so bitter. Why was she acting like that? This was a mean woman who spent her energy probing into other folks' business and that was not appropriate. Did she know that she was getting on people's nerves?

Elder Bryant was a calm man. He was in his fifties and had been married for more than twenty years. He was a family man who spent many hours counseling and working with the youth. After raising two college graduates, he gave back to his community through monetary donations to worthy causes, including the Girls and Boys Club. He was a handsome man with distinguishing gray hair on the front of his hairline. He had smooth, black wavy hair that looked processed, but was a nice grade of hair from his mother's side of the family who were Cherokee Indians. He smiled often, though he was soft-spoken. Slow to anger and not easily intimidated, people knew that he was a man of strong principles and a person of sound character who spoke for those who could not speak for themselves. He was a proud graduate of Morehouse College. Through his sponsorship, he had sought out and helped five high school students in the past four years receive full scholarships to attend the college he loved.

"I don't mean any harm, but I say what I mean." Sister Clay was not giving up.

Just as Elder Bryant was about to speak, Elder Grant

interrupted. "I don't think we need to expand on this topic because it is important that members keep up the church through their time and donations. It takes a lot of money and time to keep the church repaired and maintained. It is the members' responsibility to work with the pastor, elders and deacons to get things done. The pastor cannot do these things himself. I do believe that it is irresponsible to think otherwise. I do hope and pray that each of you come to the business meeting, hear what the repairs are and vote on the repairs according to your heart."

With that, the discussion was over. Sister Clay was pissed. Those frown lines she had earlier at church returned and her lip had curled up like she could smell something unpleasant on the tip of her nose. She raised her hand to her forehead and with the index finger of her right hand; she rubbed the right side of her temple. Mother and I stood up and started clearing the table. Everybody moved to the living room and discussed the sermon from earlier. For the first time that day, Sister Clay was speechless. Yet, even without talking, I could see her mind moving and knew that something else was brewing in that busy little head of hers.

Chapter 5

My life was complicated. Dad had died while I was working on my master's degree. My mother handled his death well. She was a faithful church member and followed God's commandments. Therefore, she was able to handle the death of the man she had been married to for more than thirty years.

When my dad, William, met mother, she was living on her own, struggling to raise her little sister. Mom had custody because her own parents died at a young age, leaving her to care for their young child. Dad saw Mom at the corner store, trying to purchase groceries, but she did not have enough money to get everything she had put onto the counter. He paid for the groceries and then told the storeowner that Mother had the authority to come and use his credit to buy things whenever she wanted to. After that incident, they were together until he died.

Dad had been a solid man. He was a good father, who did not spare the rod. My siblings and I tried to do the best we could to stay out of trouble, because Dad ruled with a strong arm and nobody wanted to suffer his wrath. He had worked at Ford Motors on the assembly line.

Dad was a thick man, not skinny and not fat. He was good looking and wore his clothes well. From the moment my parents started dating until their marriage; Dad never strayed or had an affair as far as mother knew. My siblings and I were raised with the understanding that marriage was sacred and adultery was not acceptable. Therefore, once I discovered that Darren was married, I should have ran as fast as a lion through the jungle, but I didn't because it was too late. I was in love.

Darren Tate was a Math professor. He was a handsome man who almost had that rugged look. He liked wearing blue jeans with a long sleeved shirt and a necktie. On the day we met, he was wearing his Timberland boots. He looked professional, but had two days' worth of stubble on his face. He walked over to me and introduced himself. The man had me mesmerized in less than five minutes. It never occurred to me to ask him if he was married. I gave him my phone number and we dated ever since that day. Two years later, I had to let him go, but I was in a lot of pain. I really loved that man, but could no longer continue seeing him, knowing that he was married and had children. I decided there was no man worth burning in Hell for, but I couldn't seem to stop crying for him.

As I sat at my computer and read my email, the phone rang. When I picked it up, it was Darren. He was calling me from Southern Illinois University at Edwardsville. He wanted to see me, but I refused.

"I don't understand how you think you can walk away from me. I love you and I need you." Darren grew agitated because he wasn't used to things not going his way.

"No, Darren, I will not see you. You lied to me. For two years you played me. You knew you didn't intend to become my husband. You deceived me and you were playing around on your wife, how can I ever trust you again?"

"You can trust me because I love you and you love me. I told you my wife and I are getting a divorce. I just need more time."

Enraged, I stood up and pushed the black leather chair

over. "You told me after she did. After you were caught. You've had enough time. You have wasted two years of my life. No more, Darren, will I allow you to use me."

"I'm not using you. Let me come over and talk to you." Darren's voice sounded strained. He was upset and I could hear his voice peaking the more he talked. He was getting louder like booming thunder.

"No, Darren, leave me alone." Frustrated, I slammed the phone in his ear, knowing that if we talked longer, I would become weak. I always heard the flesh was weak and now I was a witness.

I stood in the middle of the room, wiping the tears away. I grabbed the chair I had turned over while talking to Darren, set it back upright, sat back down and continued reading my email. After spending over an hour on the computer, I decided to take a shower and retire to bed. As I walked toward the bedroom, the doorbell rang. I ran into the front area of the house, peeped through the peephole and there stood my knight whose armor seemed so shiny and pristine, but now was tarnished and dented due to the deceit he had fed me. Now I knew he was not my man, he was another woman's husband. I grabbed the doorknob and swung the door open so fast, a whisk of air floated inside the hallway.

"What do you want from me?"

"I just want to love you." With that, Darren pushed his way through the door. He grabbed and kissed me passionately, my knees buckled and that was all she wrote. Darren lifted me up and carried me to the bedroom. The passion in that room alone could melt the curtains off the wall. I was with another woman's husband and couldn't stop my desire to lie underneath him and feel his member inside of me. The feeling was overwhelming.

"I love you so much, Denise. I promise I will make it right with you."

"I can't keep doing this. It's wrong." As we kissed, his hands roamed over my body. Our clothes dropped to the floor. He lifted me up into his arms, never taking his lips off me. I felt so much love radiating from him and wanted him so bad that I begged him to enter me. "Take me now."

We made love most of the night, and then finally fell asleep. I woke Darren up near midnight and we made love again. Afterward, he pulled me close to him. With my back to him, I spooned with the man I thought I truly loved. As he kissed my neck, tears flowed down my face.

"Are you crying, Denise?" He squeezed me tighter to his body.

I didn't say a word and let the tears silently fall. He turned me to face him. Darren kissed me over and over again. He said he loved me. As he looked deeply into my eyes, he whispered, "I promise, soon we can be together."

I wanted to believe him and to forget about his wife and two children. But as I lay there holding him like he was my man, guilt consumed me. I needed God to help me. I could not do this one alone. I knew from the top of my head to the bottom of my feet that my heart was playing a game with my eternal life and I was losing.

I didn't want to sin. It didn't start that way. But after finding out Darren was married, I felt stuck and continued to allow him to perpetrate a fraud. I was too smart not to check him out. All I had to do was Google him. I had his cell phone number, his office number and believed him when he said he did not have a home phone. Darren explained that it didn't make sense to have a house phone. He claimed his cell phone was used as his house phone, too. I believed it because so many people were using one phone now, their cells.

The problem with people utilizing one phone was that men could deceive women like me who were single and looking for love. The main clue that a man was married was thrown out the window because of cell phones. In the past, when a man would not give a woman his home phone number, that was a big red flag that he had something to hide, and in Darren's case, it was a whole family.

Positioned in Darren's strong arms, I reminded him, "It's time for you to go."

"I know, baby. I'm going to take a quick shower first."

Darren jumped out of the bed, kissed me, and then went to turn the shower on. I lay in bed crying, asking God to give me the strength to do the right thing. I pleaded with God to help me stop fornicating and to stop craving and sexing another woman's husband. I uttered to the heavens, "Forgive me, God, for lusting, fornicating and committing this sin."

Chapter 6

Most of the week went smooth. I talked to Darren every day, but was true to my word of not letting him near me. If I was going to be free, he had to be avoided. I spent the week working hard and helping my staff plan a summer activity for the parents in the program. As I worked on a budget for the program, the phone rang. I picked it up and answered.

"Hello, sweetheart."

"Hi, Mom, how are you?" I laid my ink pen down on the desk.

"I'm fine. I wanted to remind you of the church business meeting on Sabbath evening. You know that you are still a member even though you have been away from the church for a while."

"Well, I am not thinking about that right now." I picked the ink pen back up and started doodling on a piece of paper.

"Honey child, you need to. All the trouble that's happening in the world, in order to survive you need a strong relationship with God."

"I know that."

Being a strong African-American woman, Mom was not about to stop her witnessing to me. "You know a lot of young people are leaving this earth so fast. I have never in my life seen what is happening in this world today. Folks are having heart attacks; children are being raped and kidnapped. Even pregnant women are being kidnapped and killed for their babies. Now you know that's a shame. I don't know who wants to have more of these bad kids?"

I laughed hard. She was right about that one. Too many bad kids wanted things without working for them. They wanted fancy cars, houses and money without completing their education. Not that all kids were smart-mouthed, but many talked back to adults and they didn't respect the elderly. *Yes, we are seeing many signs that the world and the people are colder and lack love and emotions.*

"You hear me talking to you?" Mom's voice elevated to a high-pitched sistah-girl tone. I imagined Mom standing up, being sassy while posing with her hands on her hips.

"Yes, Mother, I was just thinking about what you said." I rubbed my right temple.

"Well, don't waste all your time thinking, be a doer, and get to doing. Take action. You know what I mean?"

I chuckled. "Yes, I do."

"You are not still seeing that man, are you?"

Drumming my fingers on the desk and wanting to avoid the question, I paused before responding, "Not really."

She moaned as if she was in pain. "Oooh, Denise, you know how God feels about that?"

"I know, Mom. I'm working on it."

"Pray about it, baby. God answers prayers. Well, I'll see you on Sabbath at church and you'll attend the church meeting, right?" Mom didn't wait for an answer. "We need you young people to start learning how to run these churches. We are getting old and we won't be able to do all that we do now."

"I know, Mom. I'll see you Saturday."

"Goodbye."

"Goodbye." Hanging up the phone, I smiled thinking about mother. She was a sweet woman who had a mean streak whenever people made her angry, which wasn't often. Mom could be your biggest ally or your worst enemy, though the latter never happened. I loved that woman who nursed me when I was sick and supported me through all my activities. No matter what it was, dancing as a pom-pom girl, twirling batons as a majorette, or saying a speech, Ms. Betty Reese was going to be right there and everybody knew it. So if she wanted me to come to a board meeting, so be it, I would be there.

I left the office after saying goodbye to the staff. As I headed to the car I stopped. There standing by my car was Darren. I just stood there unsure whether to run or go forward. I was scared! When I was near him I couldn't resist him. It had been a week since we'd made love, but I was accepting his calls. I was trying to break it off, but I couldn't do it if I saw him, yet I needed to hear his voice.

Walking toward me with his arms stretched out to hug me, Darren smiled and mouthed, "Denise, I miss you."

I walked closer to the car because I didn't want anyone to

hear our conversation as people left their offices to go home for the day. Using my keypad I clicked off my car alarm and popped up the trunk to put my briefcase in.

"Darren, why are you doing this to me?" I closed the trunk and walked back to the driver's side of the car. "You are married with a family. Stop! Please! Just leave me alone."

I got into the car as he grabbed my arm. "Denise, I need to say something. I love you. I do. Please calm down."

I snatched my arm from his grip and started the car. He reached inside and pulled the key out of the ignition. Bending down, he said, "I know you don't believe me, but I love you. I know I'm a married man, but I need more time to explain things to my wife. If you were in the same situation, you wouldn't want me to pull the rug from under you either." He clutched my right hand and slid a 3-carat diamond on my finger. It was beautiful. The stone was a princess cut and it looked great on my finger, shining as the sun's rays touched it. Now that was too deep. Putting that ring on my finger proved that Darren loved me. He confirmed that his intention was honorable. He had told me so many times before we would get married. But today, he proved it. He put his head through the car window and kissed me to seal the deal. I was speechless, but felt the happiness boiling in the pit of my stomach.

"I'll be by around seven and I'll bring dinner." He kissed me again, smiled and walked off. With that one act, he calmed me for a moment. I sat in the car for about five minutes, unable to move. I was engaged to a married man. Having a ring answered my question about his love for me. That was a major step. Our love was real.

As I drove out of the parking lot, I sang, "I got a rinnng, I got a rinnng."

When Darren arrived at seven o'clock, we ate and retired to bed. I don't remember much about the evening, but know that my toes were curling and I was hoarse from all the screaming I'd done. Darren did not do any better, for I'd scratched his back up. I had fallen right back into a bad habit and had lost the ability to fight a losing battle with the devil.

****

Sabbath was a beautiful day. I waited all week to visit Mother and finally it was Saturday and after church we had an opportunity to talk. Since I lived in the county area of Missouri called Spanish Lake, a nice quiet area, I visited Mom once or twice a week. Due to the distance and a busy schedule, it was always customary for me to visit on a Saturday or Sunday.

The sun was shining bright and it seemed that the rays were beaming magical sparks that were piercing hot. Once the rays hit the ground, it seemed they bounced from the ground and sprinkled small beams of heat that spanked anyone outside from head to toe. The heat whipped our butts and was hot enough to make anyone realize that if Hell was that hot, there was no way that you would want to visit it.

When I arrived at church, the first person I saw was my best friend, Ms. Clay. She bum-rushed me. "Where is Betty?"

"Mother will be here soon, I guess."

"I enjoyed the dinner and conversation last week. Are we having dinner again today?"

I pushed some strands of lose hair behind my ear. "I doubt that seriously."

"Well, the pastor is preaching today. You should sit closer to the front so that you can see for yourself how attracted he is to you."

That did it. I pivoted around and said, "Sorry, I need to speak to someone." I tried to walk away, but Ms. Clay was so close to me that she stepped on the heel of my shoe, causing me to walk out of it. I was pissed. I had to ask God to move the devil out of me because I wanted to go off on that woman. As I turned back in Ms. Clay's direction, it must have appeared as if smoke was coming out of my nose because Sister Clay jumped back as if I had swung at her, which I wanted to do. The thing was my mother had never raised her children to be disrespectful to others, especially an adult. Plus, I was a professional with a reputation to uphold. But honestly, that woman was trying my patience and she was bringing something out of me that I didn't like or understand. *Lord, help me handle this woman, please.*

I turned around and saw Pastor Davis next to me. He picked up my shoe and helped to put it back on. It was a *Cinderella* moment. Unfortunately, nosy Sister Clay had witnessed it. Though it was nothing to most people, to her it was the hottest news of the day. What I didn't realize was how fast she would spread that little scene.

The services went great and the pastor spoke well. His main point was that Jesus died for us and that we should love ourselves enough to be open to love others. He said we should remember that if Jesus could love all of us and died, we could keep God's commandments.

As the choir sang, "Oh, How I Love Jesus," I looked around at the congregation, but didn't see Brother Johnson. He was the man who hollered out at the last service. I just had this awful expectation that he was going to say something negative again. When he didn't holler out, I was relieved.

After service was over, I walked up to the pastor to shake his hand. I felt eyes piercing the back of my head. I turned to look and saw the Piss Patrol. They were called the "Piss Patrol" because they were an angry group of women who always wanted to fight the members of the church. They were known for gossiping and the ring leader, Trisha Coates, was the worst. Too many times they had been in counseling with the pastor, but he wasn't successful; therefore, the Women's Ministry team was assigned to mentor them. However, they proved that they were some hard nuts to crack. The five of them stood near a corner, staring at me. They all had on miniskirts and stiletto shoes. Out of the five, two had the bodies to wear that kind of attire. The other three girls' blouses were rising up and their stomachs were showing. Two of them had visible stretch marks left from having their babies too young, possibly in high school. Deanna, the second in command, was standing like she was a hooker with one leg pointing toward the right and the other leg pointing in front of her. If she moved, her shirt would split right down the middle. They were smacking their gum and blowing bubbles.

Head usher, Sister Martin, went over to ask them to stop talking so loud in the sanctuary. Trisha busted a bubble in response. I heard Deanna say, "She thinks she is going to get him, but it ain't happening." I guessed Sister Clay had already started spreading the rumor.

I turned around and bumped into the pastor. "Hi, Pastor. That was a wonderful sermon and helpful. Thank you."

"Thank you, Sister Reese. When you have a moment I would like to speak to you about doing work with our teens. I hear that you have a wonderful relationship with our teens and the ones in the city."

I looked at the pastor and bit my bottom lip. "Sorry Pastor, I haven't worked with teens this year. Last year I had a weekly rap session in St. Louis, but I haven't been active this year."

"Can we discuss it further later?"

"That will be fine."

I walked out the door and was standing on the sidewalk, talking to my sister, Terri, when the Piss Patrol came out of the church. They were talking loud and smacking gum. Trisha rolled her eyes at me. I chose to turn my head; they were not worth the hassle.

Sister Clay walked out the door and saw Terri and me talking, she backed into the church as if I didn't see her. She knew that she had started something; she didn't want to face me. It was the same old thing that people who start trouble always do, which is throw a rock and hide behind their hand.

As we continued to chat, I noticed that the Piss Patrol was

still standing near.

"I don't know what the pastor sees in her anyway 'cause she ain't all that!" Trisha said this with emphasis. She was rolling her neck with her hands on her hips.

At first I stared at that group of common-sense-challenged girls and laughed. Terri was a bit more direct. "Do y'all need something?" The response received was the sound of heels clicking on the pavement as they walked away. They weren't tough after all.

We were still laughing when I noticed how beautiful my sister was. She was in her third year of college, majoring in Electrical Engineering, and she was achieving at a high level academically. I was so proud of her.

Before we could leave, Pastor Davis returned and handed me a card. I bent to see what was on the card, when he said, "Would you mind calling me? I have something else to discuss with you."

"I will call you tomorrow, Pastor."

"That will be great."

We checked him out as he walked away. "He's handsome," I announced.

Terri turned her head to watch, "You got that right. Girl, you know how we do. You should see what's up with him!"

"I have eyes for one man. Sister Clay can stop all her

gossiping and get herself a life because I'm not interested. The Piss Patrol can take a shopping trip to the mall because they need one."

We cracked up laughing and left to have dinner with Mother.

After dinner and socializing with Mother and Sarah, we prepared for the church board meeting. The meeting would start immediately after sundown. I wasn't even sure why I was attending, but decided it was to pacify my mother. Terri opted to go out with her friends.

When we exited the house, I smelled something. "What is that smell, liquor?"

"I don't smell anything." Mom looked around the room as if she would see a liquid bottle drinking itself. She rushed her friend out the door. Sarah didn't say a word.

Mom and Sarah Connors had been friends for more than forty years. They went shopping at least once a week, sometimes twice. They confided in each other about everything. Sarah was a widower. She had one daughter who lived in California. She visited her once a year. Sarah did not like to fly, so she limited her visits. But she missed her grandchildren and her child. She appeared so lonely. She spent a lot of time with Mom. As a social worker, I decided to pay a little bit more attention to her. I could've sworn she went into the bathroom and came back out smelling like liquor.

We rode together to church and dropped Sarah off at home. Sarah lived about five miles from the church. During the whole car ride, Sarah had become extremely talkative. As she talked, the scent of alcohol increased and I could smell a light wisp of liquor in the breeze of air drifting into the car from the open window. However, I wouldn't testify on a stack of Bibles what the smell was.

Once back at the church, Pastor Davis called the meeting to order. Everyone was silent, but I could feel something ugly in the air when Brother Johnson ambled through the door. Mother said that Brother Johnson was bitter about not being selected to hold an office in church. She explained that there were many folks who felt slighted and were sulking.

Once a year, at the business meetings, people were nominated by the church members to sit on the nomination committee. This was an important position to have; a group of individuals who were nominating members to serve in key positions of the church. Those individuals who were selected to serve as the director or coordinator of a particular department would also sit on the church board. So it was an honor to have what most felt were the top positions in the church. Not only were you a valuable member of the board who made decisions for the church, you were also privy to confidential members' information, church decisions, and any problems that the committee was charged with solving. If you were one who was good at starting problems in the church or seen as negative or even participating in activities not becoming of a Christian, you would not receive a nomination to hold a position.

The problem was that many of the members saw it as a coveted church role to have. They became angry, cliquish and downright mean when they did not receive the position that they had planned to secure. Many times after the nomination committee concluded its assignments, there were many problems. If a gossiper or troublemaker was selected, they would leave the confidential meeting and discuss whatever was said. Sister Clay sat on the committee two years ago and since that time the church had been going through a lot of problems. She left a meeting and discussed why certain members were not accepted and awarded positions. She divulged sensitive information, leaving many hurt and confused. The church was still healing after that.

"Mom, I'm not looking forward to this meeting. I hate to see members at odds with each other."

"You know sometimes it's all right to have healthy discussions. As members, we have to learn to behave like Christians when there are conflicts." Mom pointed to the front of the church and my eyes followed.

"See that guy. He became so upset because he failed to receive a nomination; he removed his jacket and tried to fight a couple of members."

"That is so pitiful. People need to focus on God, not positions and other things."

"I know. But many of us are getting there. It takes having a strong relationship with God. That takes work, honey."

As we sat, waiting to receive the agenda for the meeting, Sister Clay walked in with Trisha and her crew following right behind her. It was a shock to many to see Sister Clay hanging around Trisha because she was at least twenty-five years older than her. Sister Clay was in her mid-forties while Trisha was twenty years old. They made an odd couple. I believe when you love negative stuff and gossip, you like being around those who partake in it. My mother always said that all birds of a feather flock together. In this instance, it was proven.

Pastor Davis discussed the need for the church to have repairs done. He said that the roof had sprung a leak, the sanctuary needed carpet and several of the offices needed air conditioning. As he discussed the three bids that he had secured, Brother Johnson raised his hand to ask a question.

Pastor Davis acknowledged him. "Yes, Brother Johnson."

Brother Johnson stood up. "Pastor, I want to know where all the money has gone. This church is running through our building fund like water, yet I don't see any work that is worthy of the kind of money that's been spent." Brother Johnson pulled both of his pants legs up by the knees and sat back down.

"Brother Johnson, as the pastor of the church, I have a set limit of spending with the board's approval. I have a five-hundred-dollar expense account. Outside of that, all repairs and requests that exceed the five-hundred dollars must go through the board for approval and then to the church body, at a business meeting, to get final approval. No money is spent without church approval."

"Pastor, you are abusing us. You are overspending and misappropriating the church money and I don't appreciate it." Mr. Johnson turned around to get others to back what he was saying. Suddenly, another man jumped up and asked the pastor to give an account of the expenditures for the church.

The church secretary grabbed her huge binder and started

flipping through the pages. As she flipped through the pages, she held up her finger to let the pastor know that she wanted to speak. She turned to look at Brother Johnson with an utter look of disgust on her face. With her teeth clenched, she said, "Pastor Davis and church members, I have every memo and all the minutes of every item that has been approved by the church. I don't like it when unsubstantiated accusations are made. Brother Johnson, you are going to go down in fiery hell, talking to the pastor with such disrespect."

"Sister Baxter, please sit down. You are the pastor's flunky," Brother Johnson said as he laughed out loud.

"I don't appreciate that, Brother Johnson. You are a troublemaker and we should not be having a conversation like this." She slammed her binder on the pew.

Jumping back up, Brother Johnson got louder and started waving his hands in front of him. "I am sick of this stuff. I want accountability of church funds."

"Brother Johnson," Brother Simmons said, trying to attain a sense of control in the meeting, "you are out of order and I personally think you should leave until you calm down."

"Make me leave, Brother Simmons." Brother Johnson started taking off his suit jacket and rushed toward Brother Simmons.

The men practically pulled Brother Johnson out into the church vestibule. When they returned they were without Brother Johnson. But that was just the start of the church members' arguments.

Pastor Davis called the church to order. He asked the church to pray with him, but before they could start, Trisha from the Piss Patrol jumped up and said that she had heard that a member of the church was involved in fornication at the church, and she wanted to know if it was true.

This is what I was talking about to mother. When I came to church it was because I needed a Christian experience, and wanted to be revitalized to go back to work and act like a person who had sense and loved her fellow man/woman. I needed a spiritual connection because where there is much prayer, there are better results.

Leaning over to speak to Mother, I asked, "Is this what you wanted me to come here for? This is stupid and so unchristian like. What did I tell you about churches with cold-hearted members? I could have gone to the club to see this crap."

"Well, you didn't go to the club. This is God's house; He will work this out."

Looking at Mother, I knew that she believed He would, so I sat back and waited to see what would happen next. Now, Trisha wanted to know who was doing who in the church. This was going to be interesting.

The pastor looked up to the ceiling as if he was pleading with God to intercede. I followed his eyes and looked up, too. When he brought his head back down and looked into the audience, he saw me and smiled. My lips stretched out into a magnificent smile that spread from corner to corner. For some strange reason it felt nice to have him acknowledge me.

"Pastor, did you hear what I asked you? I heard Sister Barnes was having sex with Deacon Blue. Shouldn't they be exonerated from the board? They not married."

"Sister, tonight we are discussing church repairs. What you are asking is not your business. If someone wanted their business in an open forum, they would have brought it here. That question is inappropriate and as Christians, we are not supposed to be spreading rumors about members in this church."

Brother Simmons said, "The word is dismissed or expunged; means to eliminate. You know, like some of you members want to do to some of the good folks here."

Sister Baxter reminded the church that the pastor wanted to pray and that we should've all been kneeling. Trisha and the Piss Patrol huffed, puffed and walked briskly out of the church.

I laughed. This was too funny. Who did those girls think they were? They acted like others should've bowed down to them.

As the church kneeled, the pastor prayed for guidance, compassion for others, cooperation and love amongst the congregation. His prayer was so powerful that when everyone sat back on the pews, there was a new spirit inside the church. It was the spirit of cooperation and love. People started talking to each other with respect. The pastor had established order in the church. As the church continued meeting I stood up, grabbed my purse and walked out to get a breath of fresh air.

In the vestibule stood three teens who appeared puzzled and confused with pasted frowns displayed on their pretty faces. They had heard the commotion in the church.

"Ms. Reese, were Brother Simmons and Brother Johnson fighting in the church?"

"Why, did you all see them fighting?"

The first teen said, "No, we heard them cutting up like little kids."

The second teen said, "The grown-ups in this church are so stupid. They are so embarrassing."

I was trying to think of something intelligent to say that would help them. "The grown-ups are struggling to be Christians, too. Just like the devil tempts children and teens, he does the same thing to adults."

"Yeah, but adults should know better." The first teen slapped her hand against the second teen's in a high-five.

"We all have to pray daily for God to help us avoid the devil's temptations. None of us are exempt. So I will be praying for everybody here, the teens, myself and the adults."

I hugged the teens, and then walked to the ladies' room. When I returned to the sanctuary, the church members were calm and working together. They continued the meeting as I sat there thinking about the way things had transpired. I had never attended a church meeting where folk were about to fight and the only thing that could stop them was two men.

Otherwise, things would have gotten ugly.

What most people don't realize is this, if you are a weak or struggling Christian, things like that can set you way back. I was having a hard enough time with my life without church involvement and now that I was tiptoeing my way back into the church, doubt was everywhere in my mind and heart. I sat in the meeting, thinking that being with a man who was not my husband was better than fighting and causing problems in the church.

I had watched a group of girls sass the pastor and embarrass most of the church members with their silly antics. I saw people disrespecting each other and making unsubstantiated claims against one another. But I had to admit, the pastor was strong, smart, prayerful and serious about the business of the church. He was a brave, loving pastor whose eyes looked lonely and in need of compassion and love. Watching the pastor made me look at things differently; it almost made me feel attracted to him. But I prayed that God would work on me and the church members. If I didn't know anything else, I knew I didn't want to be lost.

Chapter 7

Sunday was my sleep-in morning. I worked from Monday through Friday and had attended church for the past three Saturdays. Now, my plan was to sleep and wash clothes. As I tossed and turned in bed after my beautiful, sexy dreams, I woke up because my new diamond ring from Darren somehow got caught in my bedspread. As I tried to pull it from the threads, the phone rang. I picked it up rather quickly.

Agitated, I answered, "Hello?"

"Good morning, may I please speak to Sister Denise Reese?"

"This is she." I wondered who it was. I knew it was someone from the church because they were calling me Sister, but I had answered my bedroom phone, which did not have caller ID.

"Sister Reese, this is Pastor Davis. Did I wake you?"

"Good morning, Pastor. No, you didn't wake me," I said, as I sat upright in the bed.

"Do you have a minute to talk?"

"Yes. What can I do for you?"

"You know, Sister, yesterday I mentioned to you about working with our teens. I've heard a lot about you and your history with working with teenagers throughout the community. Our teens are in need of someone who can share resources and help encourage them."

"Pastor Davis, I am not sure that I am the right person for that. As you may have heard, I haven't been attending church in years. So coming back right now is something I am trying to do, but I still have other things in my life that I need to work on."

"I understand. The other things in your life, do you need any help in dealing with them?"

"I'm trying to handle them. I will be okay."

"Also, I'd like to invite you to a cookout at my house next week with the elders, deacons and some of the teens and other members who I have asked to work with the youth."

I vacillated before I responded. "I'm not sure."

"Sister Reese, I will not put pressure on you. However, we would love to have you attend." He paused in anticipation of my answer.

"When and what time?"

"It will be at my home, next Sunday at four o'clock. Do you have something to write with?"

"Yes." I grabbed a pen and paper off the nightstand and asked him for the information. I wrote down his home address.

"Sister Reese, I look forward to seeing you."

I became silent. I didn't want him to get any ideas. Sister Clay had me going with her gossiping.

Finally, I answered in an octave above a gentle whisper, "Thanks, Pastor. I'll see you next week."

After I hung up the phone, I laid back in bed. I wanted to enjoy my day, but that wasn't going to happen. The phone rang once again.

Snatching the phone off its base, I said in a harsh low tone, "Yes?"

"Christians don't answer the phone like that, young lady. Did you have a rough night or something?"

Oh no, Sister Clay isn't calling me after that stunt she pulled at church! This woman has a lot of nerve! I am going to have to get this lady straight real fast.

"Sister Clay, what can I do for you and why are you calling me this early? Or better still, why are you calling me at all?"

"I know you have been out of church for a while, but Sister Reese that is not how you greet your sister in Christ."

"Is that right? You are my sister in Christ after that stuff you started at church? I do not appreciate you spreading rumors and innuendos about me." One of my strengths was my truthfulness. I called things as I saw them. I believed in not waiting to fix a problem.

"All I said was the pastor was attracted to you. I wasn't lying. You know a blind man can see that."

"What's wrong with you? I have been at that church three times and for you to start a rumor like that about the leader of the church is wrong and you will have to answer to God about that."

"God knows that Pastor Davis is attracted to you and so do other church members."

"You know what, Sister Clay, there are no reasons that I can think of that you should be calling me. You haven't asked me to participate on any church committees and we're not friends, so why have you called me?"

"You know, they said you are bougie and think you are better than others. But I defended you. I told those sisters that you are a sweet young lady, but maybe I was wrong."

"God don't like ugly and He is not too crazy about pretty, so I think you need to tread lightly, pretending to do God's work, but doing malicious things to people who are trying to live right."

"I'm just trying hard to show my love. You are the one who is hard to get to know."

"Sister Clay, maybe this is not the right time for us to continue this conversation. So let's call it a day and I'll talk to you later."

"Sister, I would like to pray for you."

What? This lady is off her rocker. First, she starts all these rumors about me, but then she wants to pray for me? No way! It is not happening. Not today or tomorrow.

"Sister Clay, maybe some other time, I'll talk to you later."

Relieved to hang the phone up, I sat in bed, thinking. As I thought about my life and how I met Darren, I smiled.

I knew that I was going to have to change my ways. I was from a healthy family who believed in honoring marriage vows and since I told my mom about me dating a married man, it was something too hard for me to live down with her. I didn't choose to fall in love. It was something that just happened. I was not looking for love, love found me.

I decided to get up out of the bed, since my time had been interrupted by Pastor Davis and Sister Clay. I decided to shower and slip on a pair of navy jogging pants and my orange-and-blue reunion T-shirt from my alma mater, East St. Louis Senior High School. I wanted to be comfortable as I cleaned the house and cooked an oatmeal breakfast, which I did infrequently. As I was dusting the living room end tables, the phone rang. "Hello?" There was no answer. "Hello?" Still nothing. But I heard light breathing. I hung up. If anything pissed me off, it was people calling my home and breathing on the phone. If you don't have the courage to talk to people, why call? People do the stupidest things. I mean, I did that crap when I was in high school. As an adult, I found that stuff so juvenile. "Get a life," I mumbled to myself about the caller.

I continued to clean the house. Since I had only eaten oatmeal and drank tea for breakfast, my stomach was letting me know that dinner was needed soon. A growl deep down roared so loud, it almost scared me. I walked through the kitchen and decided to find something to cook for dinner. I opened the refrigerator and pulled out a pack of chicken wings. Placing them in a bowl of water, I turned the stove on and checked the cabinets for something to go with the meat. As I grabbed a can of string beans and a box of Minute Rice, I stumbled and dropped the food because the ringing of the phone scared me. Rushing to pick it up, I hesitated for a second before I said, "Hello?" There was no sound. "Hello?" That pissed me off. "Hello. What do you want?" Again, there was no answer. "Okay, you are going to make me lose my religion. I am going to cuss you out." Bang! The caller slammed the phone hard in my ear. "Stupid. Ooooh," I said, balling my fist as if the caller was there for me to knock some class into him or her.

I picked up the can of green beans and the box of rice I dropped and finished cooking and cleaning the house. I decided that after I ate dinner I would soak in the tub to relax. Full from eating, I walking through my home, I went in the guest bathroom and ran a tub full of water. While the water was running, I took off my clothes and grabbed a silk robe. I put as much Sweet Vanilla bubble bath as I could into the water without it bubbling over onto the floor. *Ooooh, that looks great.* Just as I dropped my robe and put my big toe in the water to assure that it was the right temperature and not too hot, the doorbell rang. Grabbing my robe and putting it back on, I went to the door and peeked out the side window pane. It was my baby.

He looked gorgeous and sexy. He was wearing a pair of black jeans and a black muscle T-shirt. I opened the door and he walked in and picked me up. We kissed a long time before I grabbed him and took him into my bedroom. I had never held a man that tight in my life. I felt so comfortable and so loved. He made love to me for what seemed like hours. As we lay together, kissing and snuggling, the phone rang again. Although I had caller ID, it was apparent that the person was blocking out their number. "Darren, someone has called several times today and they are just breathing on the phone."

He held me tighter. "Just a prank caller, don't worry."

"I'm not worried. I just think it's stupid and I wonder if it is someone I know."

"I doubt it, Denise. If it was, they would say something."

"I guess you are right."

"I'm always right," he said as he pulled me back to him and started nibbling on my ear. Turning me toward him, he slipped his tongue into my mouth.

"I'm starving."

"You want me to order something?"

"Darren, I already cooked," I said as I climbed out of the bed. Darren followed. We went into the bathroom, refreshed my tub with new heated water, bathed each other and headed to the kitchen, wrapped in towels.

We ate dinner, went back to my bedroom, made love again, and then slept late into the evening. I woke him up at nine o'clock that night. Earlier in the day, he had asked me to wake him up at that time. "Honey, do you have somewhere to go?"

"I have to go home, that's all."

He kissed me and hopped out of the bed. As he walked away, I watched his backside. This man was gorgeous, all over. I slipped out of bed and walked into the bathroom. I pulled down the toilet cover and sat down and watched him showering through the clear curtain. He washed with unscented soap because he didn't want his wife to smell another kind of soap on his body, but he had to remove my scent off him. Another woman could smell another's scent. That would have been an obvious sign that he was cheating.

I loved that man. I knew it was wrong. If I was the wife and found out that my husband was committing adultery; I would be devastated. Yet even knowing that he was married and that I was committing a sin could not stop my heart from wanting and needing Darren. I was trying to do right, but I couldn't blame one person for how my heart pined for another woman's husband. The Bible said that we should love one another, but not to love a married man as if he was my husband. I didn't want to sin, but that sin felt so good.

After we kissed, he left. I went to my bathroom, let the water out of the tub and refilled it. I just wanted to soak and reminisce about how good Darren made me feel. I thought about that Luther Ingram song, "If Loving You Is Wrong, I Don't Want to Be Right." I sang a few lines of the song out loud. "Your friends tell you there's no future in loving a married man, if I can't see you when I want to, I'll see you when I can. If loving you is wrong, I don't wanna be right."

Chapter 8

The whole week went by fast. Nothing exciting happened. I tried reading the Bible, but I kept putting it down. I even visited some of my friends whom I had not seen in a while. I had a session with Darren who constantly assured me how much he loved me. On Friday night I laid out my clothes for church.

****

My alarm clock buzzed at eight o'clock Saturday morning. As soon as I heard it, I hit the snooze button even though I knew I needed to get up and be ready to drive the thirty-five minutes to East St. Louis, Illinois to attend church. Dozing back off again, the clock's alarm rang again. I hit the off button and jumped up. I had to find something else to wear as I decided not to wear what I had laid out.

I walked into the walk-in closet, toward my more conservative clothing. As I searched through my so-called church clothing, I pulled out a pastel pink and white suit. The jacket had three quarter sleeves and white thin lines going through it. The shirt was a solid pink. I paid more than three hundred dollars for that suit.

I laid the suit on my king-sized bed. Then I walked back into the closet to find a pair of shoes. I found a pair of nice pink sandals. Smiling to myself, I knew that I would look good, which I prided myself on doing.

I went to the bathroom, turned on the shower, and then grabbed my shower cap. I laid my lingerie on the rack and stepped into the shower. It felt so good. The water beat down on my back like little baby fists and soothed areas that were extremely stressed; I marveled in its seduction. The water penetrated my soul as it heated the coldest part of my heart, knowing that Darren may have been lying in bed with his wife. The same wife he claimed he no longer loved; the same wife he said he was going to divorce as soon as he received the new position as dean of his department. He said he had worked too hard for the position and did not want anything to affect it.

The water felt like little fingers titillating my body and warming my soul. My soul ached because I loved someone who was not mine. I tossed my head back to let the water hit spaces along my collarbone; I turned my neck to let the water penetrate the pressure points in my neck. I turned the faucet to high to make the water flow stronger and more violent. I wanted the water to beat me, torture me, and punish me. I was seeing a married man whom I knew was married. Yet, in my own defense I didn't know at first. Or did I? I knew like most women who went that route. There were plenty of signs there. I just ignored them. Even my best friend, Diana, knew.

When I first introduced Diana to the new man in my life, she had this look on her face like she knew him. The thing about Diana was she had been married before until she discovered that her husband was having an affair. Too hurt to forgive, she divorced him and moved to St. Louis, Missouri. Diana was a brilliant trial lawyer. She was twenty-nine years old and already had a track record for winning her cases. She did not have any kids, so she was able to put in long hours and travelled to interview witnesses and encourage them to return to testify. She was a beautiful lady, which helped her in the courtroom. So many of the other lawyers failed to prepare their cases to the fullest because they believed she was more into her looks than into discovering, finding and presenting a good case to the jury.

Too many times they had been fooled. Sometimes her looks worked for her on the outside of the courtroom, too. She had been successful in getting people to trust her gentleness because of her beautiful, innocent face. She was honest and true to her word, too. If she couldn't do it, it wasn't because of her lack of trying. It was because it was impossible. People trusted her because she was so real. It was that realness that caused her husband to run into the arms of another woman who was more passive and had a less-threatening job.

I met Diana Cartwright at a networking meeting. We had attended the Who's Who in Black St. Louis reception for a new book being released, which we both were being profiled in. I sat next to Diana. Most of the other people milled around with huge smiles pasted on their faces, happy to meet the news reporters, prominent politicians and other high-ranking executives who were also being celebrated for their successful work in the St. Louis Metropolitan area.

Neither Diana nor I were in the mood to be sociable, until we sat next to each other and struck up a conversation. We talked throughout the presentation, and then we exchanged phone numbers. We'd been friends ever since that day, almost four years ago.

We were the direct opposite of one another. She was about five-foot-eight and 150 pounds while I was five-foot-three and 130 pounds. She wore her jet-black hair straight down her back while my hair was sandy brown, and hung just past my shoulders. She wore business pants suits, except in court, and I wore business skirts and dress suits. I was friendlier than she was and trusted much more easily than she did. That could have been because of our experiences, too.

She arrived to my house unexpectedly two years ago and found me entertaining Darren. I introduced them before she left, claiming to have something to do. Later, she told me that she thought he was married even though she did not know him. She said she felt it in her bones. As usual, I didn't listen to her. I was in love with Darren and didn't want to hear anything that would make me doubt Darren or my love for him.

****

After showering, I dressed and left the house. I arrived in East St. Louis at 10:55, five minutes before the start of divine worship. The pastor and the elders were lined up and ready to walk into the church. Pastor Davis grasped my hand and reminded me of the barbeque the next day. Two of the elders hugged me and wished me a blessed day. I found mother and sat next to her and my sister, Terri.

Throughout the service, Brother Johnson made comments under his breath. Well, they were not exactly under his breath; I could distinguish what he had said. I couldn't understand why he still attended church there, since he hated the pastor and some of the other members.

After all the formalities in the pulpit, Pastor Davis stood up and placed his Bible on the podium. "My sermon today is about tolerance." He talked about loving your neighbors as Jesus loved us. It was an emotional sermon as so many people stood up, clapped and praised God. The soloist sang "Faith." She sang the song like she was a recording artist. I stood there crying. I knew that I needed to have faith that could conquer anything. But I was so weak. I was a sinner.

After church, a huge group of us stood around, talking about how good Pastor Davis preached. For the first time, since arriving back, I felt the Spirit of God at church. Love was in the air and it was all around us. In the group were my mother, Terri, Sarah, Elder Bryant and several other church members. We were elaborating on the service and several in the group were discussing what time they needed to visit the sick. I decided I would go too since I had not done that in several years.

Elder Bryant walked away as did several others in the group. My sister and I walked away after I had assured the others that I would meet them at three o'clock at Calvin Johnson Nursing Home. As I walked away, I noticed the Piss Patrol staring at me. I looked, but continued to walk to my car. Trisha and several others followed me to the parking lot.

"Hey, Denise, what's up?"

I didn't want to respond, but I was trying hard to be a better person. "Hi."

Pointing her finger in my direction and rolling her neck, Trisha said, "That's all you got to say? I'm trying to be nice. See, you think you better than me 'cause you driving a Lexus, but so what? I'm doing me."

My sister jumped in. "Continue doing you then and step off."

"Now, Terri, this is between me and your sister. She is trying to take my man and I don't play that."

Terri laughed. "Your man? Girl, you are really tripping. Your man? He doesn't attend this church, does he?"

Trisha was getting pissed and still rolling her neck around like she was in the hood, on the corner, getting ready to drop it like it's hot. "This is an A-B conversation, so you need to C your way out."

"Girl, that line is so tired. I'll tell you what. You need to go on before something happens here that you don't like."

Terri walked up on Trisha and I snatched her back. "Get in the car. Don't go to her level. She doesn't have a man I would even date."

"Well, stay out of the pastor's face. He ain't married and I have been checking him out long before you rolled up in here."

"Now that's funny," I said. I got in the car and laughed. I saw the anger in her eyes. She was serious. What would possess that girl to think that the head of the church had eyes for her or even me for that matter? I thought church people were going to be a little different than what I experienced on the street, but this was hilarious. I backed out and drove to mother's house.

At mother's house, Sister Clay stopped by. She was in the kitchen, telling my mother that I had been disrespectful to her. I walked in on the conversation.

"Denise, Sister Clay was telling me that you disrespected her when she called you to show sister love. Is that true?"

"Did you tell her, Sister Clay, how you were probing into my personal business?" I asked her. "I don't think I disrespected you. I was firm in letting you know that you were not my friend, so I didn't understand why you were calling inquiring about my love life. Like you, Sister, I'm an adult. I did my best to respect you."

"See what I mean? Your daughter thinks she is so high and mighty. I thought she was a sweet young lady, but she's ornery and not a good Christian. You need to teach her how to respect her elders."

I remembered the scriptures, which stated to love your neighbor as yourself. "I'm sorry, Ms. Clay, if I offended you. Please, do accept my apology."

Sister Clay snapped her fingers like she was at a poetry reading. "That's more like it," Sister Clay said, like she had won the battle.

Mom smiled and that's all I needed. I did not want Mom to become stressed. After all, that was her church and she didn't need any trouble.

"Thanks, Denise. Sister Clay, it would be wise if you would leave your conversations with Denise about church functions. I think that would stop a lot of problems."

"You're right, Betty. I didn't mean to bring this to you, but it was heavy on my mind. I guess since I am here, I can just stay for dinner. What did you cook?"

My mother was a sweet lady. She told us the menu and instructed us to go to the bathroom to wash our hands. We all did.

At the dinner table Mom asked me to say grace. I complied. "Please bow your heads. Heavenly Father, I want to thank You for the food that we are about to eat. I pray that You bless the cook who prepared the food for the nutrition of our bodies. Bless all of us who sit at the table and help us to love and respect one another. All these things I ask in Your name. Amen."

All at the table said "Amen" in unison as we picked up our silverware and proceeded to fill our plates with greens, yams, macaroni and cheese and fried chicken. Although most Seventh Day Adventists were vegetarians, we were not; there were many of us who loved meat, especially Sister Clay, who was eating as if she had not had a good meal since Christopher Columbus said he discovered America.

At the table, Sister Clay decided to lecture me. This, after all we had been through. "Denise, be careful of Trisha and her friends. The pastor and the Women's Ministry team have been counseling those young ladies for months and they are still out of control. It is going to take much prayer, guidance and Bible classes to get them to be respectful ladies."

Mom laid her fork on her napkin. "Why does Denise need to be careful?"

"You see, there is a lot of gossiping going on around the church about the pastor having eyes for your daughter. I'm sure he is tired of being single and since she is the only one not running up behind him, it seems he might be interested in her. Word has it that the elders had to meet with her because Trisha was calling Pastor Davis and it wasn't for prayer."

"That's probably a rumor and you are spreading it more by talking about." My mother was so not with it. I wanted to hear more.

Biting into her chicken breast, Sister Clay wiped the juice running down the corner of her lip. "If it is a rumor, Trisha is spreading it herself. She's the one telling everybody who will listen that the pastor is her man. So the elders, deacons and others just pretty much keep the pastor from ever being alone with her."

I agreed with the sister on that. "That's a smart move because if he denies her, she can't easily falsely accuse him of something."

"That's why the members protect him so. We want the ladies to be more Christ-like, but you know it's going to take some time. Those ladies have no training or education. Trisha dropped out of high school and she already has, I think, about three kids and she's just twenty years old. You just be careful. She was in the bathroom saying that she was going to snatch a knot in your weave. I told her that wasn't no weave you were wearing. It was your hair and I think she got more jealous and madder."

"I'm not worried about her."

"Denise has God on her side. He will take care of her." My mother looked at me and smiled. She believed it and I did, too. I may have been fornicating, but I knew that God was in the business of protecting folks.

Chapter 9

I arrived at the pastor's barbeque Sunday with Mother in tow. I was not going to the pastor's house alone. Not that I didn't trust him, I just didn't know all those people yet. The pastor lived in O'Fallon, Illinois which was about fifteen minutes from the church. His home, which was a two-story brick house, boasted a huge front porch that wrapped to the back of his house. As we walked into the front door, Elder Bryant greeted us.

"It's so wonderful to see you ladies," he said as he bent to hug Mother and then me.

I looked around the house. The pastor or whoever decorated his house had impeccable taste. The living room was decorated with a formal flair. The furniture consisted of a beige leather sofa, loveseat and chair. The leather was stunning and it was accented with light-brown wood. The wood was solid. From all indications, it looked handcrafted and was Italian leather.

As we moved through the house to go to the backyard we passed his great room. I took a moment to take in the beauty of the spacious vaulted ceiling that had an open floor plan. The floors were hardwood. The room had the most beautiful black Italian leather set with a 40-inch LCD Flat Panel HDTV.

"Denise, the pastor has a nice home."

"Yes, Elder Bryant. It is beautiful."

"There's also a family room, four bedrooms, and four full

baths. The pastor has made his home comfortable."

"Yes. This is nice, Elder. Are there many people here?"

"There are about thirty people from the church in the back. Only the board members were invited and some brought a guess or two. The board met earlier for a meeting. This summer, the pastor will host an event for the entire church. You know that will keep members from thinking that the pastor has favorites."

"That's smart. You know how some people can feel left out." I was thinking that someone like Sister Clay would have a hissy fit to find out someone had something and she was not invited. So the pastor was right to host something for his congregation.

As we walked through the kitchen, which was just as elaborate as the front of the house, I stopped to admire the cabinets. They were made of white wood and there were enough to fill up any family's kitchen needs. The cabinets designated for glassware had glass doors and all the appliances were silver.

As we moved to the back of the house, I could hear the laughter and noise coming from the backyard. I opened the door and we stepped out onto a large deck.

"Hi, Sister Denise and Sister Betty."

"Hi, Elder Grant." Mother reached out and hugged him. He then extended a hug to me, too. As he turned to lead us to the area where the pastor was, I whispered, "Mom, I sure hope this is worth the long drive I took to come here."

"I think we are going to enjoy ourselves." Mother walked over to Pastor Davis while I spoke to a couple of the board members. As I chatted, my cell phone rang. "Excuse me," I said to the ladies I was talking to, as I walked away to get privacy.

"Hello?"

"Sweetheart, where are you?"

"I'm at the pastor's house for a picnic."

"I don't like your sudden interest in going to church so much."

Annoyed, I stopped walking. I growled, "Why not, Darren?"

"Because they are going to tell you something stupid to break us up and you are going to fall for that crap."

"I can't talk, I'll call you later."

"Nah, you come home early so that you can take care of your man. I need to see you."

"Bye, Darren."

I put the phone back into my purse's cell pocket. I looked up, straight into the eyes of Pastor Davis. "Hi, Pastor."

"Hi, Sister Reese. I am so glad that you made it. How are you?"

81

"I'm fine. What about you?" Since he was standing so close, I was close enough to read his mind. I saw it for the first time. He was attracted to me. He was glowing. Ladies, you know how your mother is the first one who can tell that you are pregnant and she says, "I know you pregnant, girl, look at your bright eyes, and your skin is just glowing." Well, I knew the pastor wasn't pregnant, but the man was glowing, and not only that, he was absolutely handsome.

"Come walk with me."

I followed the pastor around as he showed me his flower bed, which was one of the most beautiful ones I had ever seen. There were roses, gardenias, morning glows, violets and petunias.

"Did you plant these flowers?"

"Yes, I did. I love to garden because I love nature and beautiful things such as flowers and trees, and..." He smiled at me. "People."

"I do, too. When I look at God's handiwork, I am impressed. I love to sit and stare at pine and evergreen trees. I like looking at water, especially large bodies of blue water, though I don't want to get in it."

I looked into his eyes. "Sister Reese, has anyone ever told you that you have the most beautiful brown eyes?"

I was smiling all over the place. You couldn't take my smile if you smacked it off. I felt comfortable with him, peaceful, like a river. "Yes. I've heard that, but not so intense."

We both laughed. As we walked toward his pool area, he took my hand and helped me up the small hill. His hands were huge, but soft. I felt safe, like if I were to fall, he would be there to soften it. We held hands for a second until we realized we were doing it. We were both feeling comfortable, yet uncomfortable.

As we gazed, speechless, into the pool, he asked, "Are you seeing anyone?"

"Yes."

Before we could say another word, someone grabbed my shoulder. "Hey, Sister Reese," Sister Clay's voice rang out.

I looked at the pastor. He knew I was uncomfortable with her, because he was, too. We didn't even know how long she'd been standing there. "Hi, Sister Clay, please don't scare me like that again. I could have fallen in the pool."

"You are kidding me right, Denise?" She looked up at me and her nostrils flared and her eyes blinked hard.

"No, Sister Clay, I wasn't kidding. It's not nice to sneak up on people like that." That lady did something to my blood. She was getting on my last nerve and I only had two left.

"Oh, I wasn't sneaking. I was walking around, smelling the beautiful flowers. Pastor, you have a beautiful home and yard and everything. How much you shell out for this house?"

"Sister Clay. That's not nice. You shouldn't ask those kinds of questions. They are not appropriate," I said as I shook my head. *This woman never gives up.*

"I have a mouth and God gave me a tongue and if you want to know something you have to ask."

The pastor laughed loud and heartily. "Sister, you are right, if you want to know something you are indeed supposed to ask. However, you have to be careful about what you ask because everybody is not as friendly or as kind with responses to questions they may feel are out of line."

"The Bible says in Matthew chapter seven, verse seven, *Ask and you will receive.* And I am asking because I want to know. I might want to move in this area."

I laughed hard. That was funny. *Sister, the only way you are moving to this area is if you hit the lottery or marry an old rich man, but I can't see that happening.*

"Excuse me, Pastor," I said, turning back to him. "I'm heading back to the barbeque."

Sister Clay followed me. "I'm sorry, Sister Reese. I didn't mean to interrupt. I was just walking around, sightseeing."

I smiled, but kept walking. I walked over to Mother and whispered in her ear about her sister in Christ. "No, she didn't, Denise."

"Yes, she did, Momma. What's wrong with her? Doesn't she know that she is a pest and a troublemaker? I just hope she doesn't walk around here spreading rumors about us. Anyway, why is she here? Is she on the board or any special committees for the youth?"

"I don't think so. I think she just showed up. I guess I'll have to talk to her."

"You do that. If I have to I'm not going to be responsible for what I'm going to say."

The rest of the evening went well. We socialized with the church members and had an enjoyable evening. The pastor was a great host. We left the house around eight o'clock. I dropped Momma off and headed across the Mississippi River to go home.

As I pulled into the driveway, Darren drove up behind me. I parked in the garage and he followed. Before I could get the garage all the way down, he pulled on my clothes and started kissing my neck. He started unbuttoning my blouse and tried to take my skirt off in the garage. I gently pushed him away and ran into the house through the garage door.

Darren kissed me. He acted as if he was starved, like he hadn't eaten or had sex in weeks. My skirt fell to the floor and I stood there naked. I wanted him as badly as he wanted me. So I unbuttoned his shirt and he helped me to pull it off. It dropped to the floor. He took me right there in the living room, standing up.

He held my face in his hands. "Denise, I love you, girl."

I didn't respond because I was thinking of Pastor Davis, not him. I was scared to speak for I may have said something wrong. I prayed and asked God to help me to be a Christian.

"You okay?"

"Yeah." I kissed his lips. I felt so confused. I loved Darren, but I loved God, too. I didn't know if I should follow my heart and keep on loving Darren, or follow God and live according to His will? Loving Darren was so easy, but losing my soul was so hard.

I walked to the bathroom and filled the Jacuzzi. Darren put on his pants and shirt and walked to the car to get out the food he'd picked up for us. He was so aroused that he left the food and took me first.

As we sat in the Jacuzzi, I lay my head on his shoulder. "I love you so much."

"I know. It won't be long. I saw my lawyer today. I wanted to find out what I needed to do. I told you I was going to divorce my wife soon."

"I hope you don't feel as if I am making you do that. I will not allow you to blame me." I lifted my head off his shoulders and looked into his eyes. Lately, I had been feeling weird, being with another woman's husband. When I found out he was married I stayed because my heart had planted vines in my soul and I had fallen in love. I couldn't leave. Then I became comfortable. I got used to him and I did not like the idea of being back out in the world unattached.

"What are you thinking about?"

"Us and where we are headed."

He swiped a strand of my hair behind my ear. "We are headed to the altar; you are going to be my wife."

He grabbed me and pulled me onto his lap. We kissed as his hands slowly moved over my body like an x-ray machine, looking for areas to pinpoint for more observation. I felt his warmth that connected from his body to mine. We became one again, the second time that night.

He slept over. His wife thought he was on a business trip. He left my bed to call her. I heard the conversation. She must have said she loved him. I heard him say, "Me, too." He put his phone down and reentered the bed where we cuddled until morning.

Chapter 10

We were entering late June. It was hot and with the heat, tempers were flying and people were displaying attitudes that were unbecoming of Christians. I drove over to East St. Louis to attend a meeting at the East St. Louis Community College, bright and early Tuesday morning. It was a grant-writing meeting. It was time for me to write grants because our company was growing fast and people were requesting that our staff participate in case staffing meetings and to sit on committees to work with their families enrolled in the programs. Our services were needed because we provided information and resources to parents to help them stabilize their families. As a director, I learned years ago that people who knew better would do better. We just needed to provide them with information and education and with that in their hands, many of our clients were progressing, finding and keeping jobs.

While in East St. Louis, I decided to stop at 25th and State to shop at a couple of the stores. I planned to visit Mother before I returned to St. Louis. As I was walking around Ashley Stewart I saw Trisha. She was by herself, but pretended like she didn't see me. That was weird because every time I'd seen her at church she was loud and obnoxious.

She was pushing clothing around the circular clothing rack. What was so weird was that she was looking at business suits. The suits were between $150 and $200. Now this was the girl who wore hoochie clothing and five-inch heels. Ever since I met her, she always had on too-tight and way too-short, inexpensive and poorly constructed miniskirts.

I walked close enough to see if she would speak. She looked

up at me with a surprised look on her face.

"Hi, Trisha."

"Hi, Denise." She went back to shifting the suits around. I walked away, but every now and then I would look up and she was staring at me. Where was the girl who was so boisterous and rude and did her best to start confrontations and fights? Where was the vibrant girl who wasn't ashamed and would strike a pose in all her cheap clothing as if she was Tyra Banks, walking the runaway in Versace clothing? I didn't know what had happened to her, but I knew it was weird not seeing her.

As she looked around the store, I noticed the salesperson staring at her as if the minute she removed her eyes, Trisha would snatch a handful of clothing and head out the door. I walked back over to speak to Trisha again.

Trying to make friendly conversation, I asked, "Trisha, you work near here?"

She stopped dead in her tracks and turned to look at me. "No, I don't. Why you ask?"

"I don't know. I was just wondering. Those are some nice suits you are looking at."

"Not really," she said as she started walking toward the front of the store to exit.

"Oh, I thought you liked them because you had been admiring them ever since I walked into the store."

She swung her arm around like she was showcasing the clothes. "This crap would not look right on me."

Moving closer to her, I advised, "Trisha, yes they would. You have a cute shape and these suits are perfect for you."

With a soft baby-like voice so unlike her, she responded, "You think so?"

"Yes, I do."

Trisha pushed past me and walked out the door. Now that told me two things. It said to me that Trisha was not as bad as she led people to believe and that she dreamed of being able to wear the kind of clothing she saw on the racks. I decided right then that if Trisha wanted better I would help her. My mother had told me that some people get trapped in their lifestyles. It's all they know. The people in her circle, as well as her neighborhood, exhibited what she had been so accustomed to seeing. She, like so many others, felt hopeless; like they did not deserve to feel special or to have much and to prosper.

One of the reasons why I went into the field of Social Services was because I wanted to be a change agent. I wanted to work with people who wanted to change and to show them that their dreams, with hard work, could be accomplished. I wanted them to work around people who they would someday believe they could become or become even better than.

What I saw in Trisha's eyes was the same thing I had seen in so many of our clients.

Someone must have told her that she would not amount to anything and what she did was turn that self-fulfilling prophesy into her reality. She chose to believe that because of her circumstances, dreams were for other people and her life, as it was, was just that, her life. If she wanted me to help her, I would.

I had a lot to think about. The pastor wanted me to work with the teens in the church, but I could not do that while I lived in sin. I wanted to work, but giving up what I had was not an option for me. I would still help Trisha if she allowed me to. But for now, The True Church Teen Leader position was out of the question.

****

The workshop was over at twelve o'clock. I decided to stop at Cracker Barrel and pick up lunch for my mom and me. As I exited the car to go into the restaurant, I passed by and spoke to Sarah. Sarah did not recognize me. "Hi, Sister Connors."

"Who are you?" She asked as she lifted her arm up in the air as if she may have to defend herself.

"I'm Betty Reese's daughter, Denise."

"Oh, hi, Denise." She put her finger in front of her lips."Shhhhhh...don't tell nobody you seen me."

"Why not, Sister Connors?" No wonder she didn't recognize me at first, I could smell the liquor. It was so strong, she was reeking in it. "Do you have someone to take you home?" I turned my head to prevent the scent of liquor from assaulting my nostrils.

She took a step toward the door and stumbled. "I'm driving, but I stopped to get a plate for later. They are so crowded and they act like they don't want to serve me."

Grabbing her elbow and guiding her safely out the door, I stated, "I'll tell you what. What if I take you home and get mother to drive your car back to you later today?"

"Would you do that?" Sarah asked while rubbing her dress down as if she was removing wrinkles.

"Yes, I would."

"Well, Lawd have mercy, I am so glad you can take me home. I was worried, you know. I had a drink. She held one finger up. "Just one little drinnnk." Sarah held that last word so long she stumbled and I had to grab her to keep her from falling.

"On that note, I think I need to take you now. You need to get this out of your system." I tried to guide her to my car, but she pushed me away and stood in front of me.

"Dance with me, girl." Sarah grabbed my hands and in front of Cracker Barrel she proceeded to try to swing me around, like I was her dance partner. She was laughing and giggling like a teenager without a care in the world. I started trying to get her to my car.

"Dance with me, Denise. I want to dance." Sarah released

my hand and grabbed this older white man and tried to force him to two-step with her. As she gripped him closer to her, his wife walked up and broke Sarah away from her husband. I knew they had to be in their late sixties or early seventies.

Sarah had the nerve to try and get smart. "Well, take your wrinkled butt on. Acting like you too good to dance with me. And another thing, your wiiiife is old."

I almost laughed. However, it was sad enough to see this woman drunk during the height of the day and drinking alone. The worst thing was that she was driving. What if she had hit someone and killed them? What if she killed herself? Or better still, killed herself and others? She was too intoxicated to be behind a car's wheel.

I had told mother that I smelled liquor on Sarah's breath several weeks earlier. Mother acted like she couldn't smell a thing. That's what happened to people when they were lonely and depressed. Drinking was a problem with senior citizens. Sarah needed intervention from my mother and her own family. One thing I knew for sure, she would not drive that car.

I took her keys and drove her home in my car.

"Please don't tell anyone that you saw me drunk. I mean, I am not drunk 'cause I didn't drink a lot, but the Bible says that our bodies are the temple of the Holy Spirit and I shouldn't be drinking. But you know how that is. Every now and then I take a drink or two to make me feel better. So Denise, shhhhhhh, don't tell."

It didn't take me long to drive her home. Once there I

helped her up the steps and opened the door. I walked her in and sat with her awhile. I even went to the kitchen and fixed her something to eat. I prepared her a nice turkey sandwich and gave her a glass of Sprite. After she finished eating, I put her in the bed, and told her that I would return later with Mother. I took her keys with me.

While I drove to Mother's, I thought about Sarah. Why was she drinking alone and so early during the day? I wondered why she was drinking at all. I knew that she was doing a lot in church and was active on several committees, but I imagined that internally she must've been depressed, maybe even lonely. She needed help because she was drinking and driving, which was a horrible, dangerous match.

I arrived at mother's house around two o'clock. After I explained her best friend's situation, Mother sat down on the couch. She looked devastated. "I told her she was drinking too much."

Mother just bent her head down as in deep thought. "I suspected it."

"I don't know if you realize this, but alcohol and substance abuse are statistically at epidemic proportions amongst the elderly. It is not reported and is undiagnosed and ignored. There are many reasons why it is undiagnosed, but more so because senior citizens are no longer active in the mainstream of society, so no one is around to notice. Seniors don't get into trouble with the law, so there's no way of being detected that way. Also, they do not cause problems in the community, so it goes unnoticed. And since many are retired, they can't lose their jobs for going to work intoxicated."

"I thought she was drinking a lot. I smelled it on her a couple of times, but I spoke to her about it and she made me believe it was on rare occasions that she took a drink."

"Mom, has Sarah suffered any grief or loss? Is she suffering from mental health issues or other health concerns?"

"She had cataract surgery and I think she was treated for mild depression after her husband died, but that was five years ago."

"It doesn't matter. She could still be sad and lonely. Do you know how to reach her daughter, Cynthia? I believe she needs to be informed. I know if it was my mother, I would want to know."

"I could call her. I do have her number here."

"Well, call her. We need to take her car back to her and check to see if she is okay. That was so scary, catching her so drunk. I shudder when I think about what would have happened had I not seen her."

"Thank God He sent you to that restaurant."

"God does know everything. I'm glad that He intercepted that one. We can grab a bite to eat after we leave Sarah's place."

Chapter 11

I left East St. Louis around ten o'clock. I didn't even realize how late it was because I was so concerned about Sarah. That was one of my major downfalls. I worried incessantly about people I cared for and sometimes I worried myself sick. I stayed over at Mother's to help her find Cynthia's phone number. We left her a message, but eventually I got tired and left.

As I drove across the Martin Luther King Bridge, I looked through my rearview mirror and saw a car following me a little too closely. I switched on my music and was singing and enjoying my ride when I noticed the same white car still following me ten miles later. *Oh well, it could be a different car.* I continued to sing and pop my fingers when my cell rang. I picked it up. "Hello?"

"Whore!"

"Who is this?"

"You will find out soon."

With that the line was disconnected. *That was creepy.* Five miles from my home, I noticed the car again. "Someone is following me," I said out loud. I began to turn corners to try to lose the person, but every corner I turned, they turned too. So I decided to drive to the police station. They were so stupid; they followed me there until I pulled into the parking lot. When they saw where they had followed me to, they sped off. An officer walked out the door and I informed him that I was being followed, so I came there.

After telling the officer as much as I could about the car, so he could keep his eyes opened for it, he followed me home. I thanked the officer, went into the house, shut the garage door and turned the alarm off. I checked the house, went back to the front door and waved the officer off.

While I checked around the house to make sure that my doors were secured the phone rang. "Hello?"

"Hi, babe, I'm five blocks away, I'll be there in a few minutes."

When Darren arrived I opened the door and let him in. Grabbing me, he kissed me hard and I kissed him back. The guilt was killing me, but not enough to stop me. I needed his arms to hold me and to make me feel safe. We made passionate love on the floor in front of my fireplace. He held and kissed me and I kept my head under his armpits. I felt safe and I didn't want him to leave. As we lay there, saying nothing, the phone rang and I jumped.

"Why are you so jumpy?" Darren turned his head and watched me.

"Hello?" There was no sound.

I slammed the phone down. "Darren, please stay tonight, please."

Jumping up, he knocked over the crystal lamp and it crashed to the floor, but it didn't break. He grabbed me and looked deep down into my eyes as I looked up to him for comfort. "What's going on?"

"Someone keeps calling and hanging up. Tonight someone followed me all the way from East St. Louis."

"You didn't let them see where you live, did you?"

"No, I drove straight to the police station. That scared them and they kept driving. A police officer escorted me home and waited to ensure that I was okay."

"That was smart of you." Kissing me on my forehead, he whispered, "I will not let anyone bother you. But I can't stay. I have to get home. If Jill becomes suspicious, she will take me to the cleaners. We have to be careful. I already stayed once this week, I can't do it again so soon."

"Darren, baby, I don't know how much longer I can do this. I miss you when you are not here and I want you so bad to be here with me all the time. I'm so tired of sharing you. Plus, Darren, what we are doing is wrong. It is against what God requires of us."

"There you go with that mess again."

"What do you mean *that mess*? Don't you believe in God?"

"Yes, I do, but I don't think God is sitting around worried about who I am seeing with all the problems in the world. I just think that wouldn't be His concern. Not who I am sleeping with."

"I'm not going there with you. You know that if we want to see Heaven there are things we need to do."

"Yeah, but right now I want you before I leave."

Picking me up and taking me to the bedroom, he worked me over good before he showered. We lay in bed and talked before he left. I lay in bed thinking that lately we had been spending a lot of time in bed. I wondered if that was all our relationship was about. I was beginning to hate myself. I jumped out of the bed and stared at myself to see if I looked dirty. I wanted to know if my sin was noticeable. I looked at every inch of my body, searching for something to show me that people knew I was sleeping with a married man. I didn't know what I was looking for, but I knew I felt dirty and sinful.

As tears rolled down my face, Darren exited the bathroom and stood behind me. He was naked. His body was beautiful like a naked god's—no marks, no fat, no inches of fat over his waistline—just muscle and beauty. He watched me.

"What are you doing, Denise?" He had a perplexed look on his face. His eyes were looking up and his head was leaning to the side.

I just stared at him through the mirror. I looked for a reflection of something. I didn't know what I was doing. I was crying and touching my body.

"What is wrong with you? I love you. Stop this now!"

He pulled on his clothes and shoes. Then he checked his phone to see if he had missed any calls. My phone rang again. I didn't budge; I stood steadfast in the mirror.

Walking behind me, Darren wrapped his arms around my

body as if he was trying to shield me from the cold and pain that was so deep in me that if he didn't spread warmth over me he would lose me. He rocked me as if I was his baby. He kissed me and told me he loved me. I believed him. "I'm gonna take care of you. Don't you worry a bit, pretty lady?"

****

Saturday I was sitting in church. I was developing a positive habit. I could not sleep the night before because of the ringing of the phone. I spent the night with Diana. She and I spent the night talking. She tried to convince me to stop seeing Darren. She reminded me of the pain of finding out about her husband and the devastation that something like that caused.

As Diana and I sat there listening to Pastor Davis preach, Diana whispered, "Not only can your pastor preach, he is seriously handsome. Please introduce me to him after service."

"He is a looker. I'll introduce him to you."

"Is that the preacher you told me about?"

I turned to whisper in Diana's ear. "Yes. But trust me, I am not his type. I have skeletons in my closet and I can't see that being good for him as a first lady, you know."

"Why isn't he married?"

"Maybe he just hasn't found the right person. The pastor's

wife has to be someone whom others look up to. She will probably spend time in the Women's Ministry group and serve as a counselor. If they found out I was sleeping with a married man, they would not have a thing to do with me." I pressed my shirt down as if I were rubbing out wrinkles and turned to look toward the pulpit.

"Well, maybe you would be perfect for him because of your experiences? But first you need to come clean for yourself. You are going to have to let Darren go. I don't trust him anyway."

"Diana, I trust him and that's enough, he is filing for a divorce."

"Yeah, I bet he is. I just hope that you don't find yourself hurt and you blame this on all men."

Leaning over to her, I whispered, "I think we better listen to the sermon."

The pastor preached about the commandments. He said we all must obey God and follow His commandments. He explained them so that we would understand that God loved us and wanted us to obey Him, but we had free will. He further stated that in addition to the commandments we must love God and seek His grace.

I had a difficult time following the sermon because Brother Johnson was blurting out negative things. When the pastor said God was asking us to come to Him, Brother Johnson said something like some of the members needed to be the first in line. I could tell that others saw him as a nuisance because no one paid attention to him. I guess the folks in the church were used to him. I had explained his actions to Diana so that she wouldn't think I was attending a crazy church or something.

As the ushers walked to each pew with outstretched arms to dismiss us, I turned and whispered to Diana, "Look who's staring at me."

"Who?" She turned full circle.

I popped her on the arm. "Trisha and her crew. You know, when she is not around them I sense that she is different and wants something better out of life. I don't think she's happy."

"She doesn't have to be. All she has to do is ask for help and most people will help."

"I know that, but people like her spend so much time hating, they can't spot folk who are willing to share their love and time to help better people."

As we inched in the line, waiting as people greeted the pastor and the elders, my mother walked over and hugged Diana. "I am so happy to see you here. I haven't seen you around the house in a while."

"I've been so busy, Ms. Reese." Diana had her arm wrapped around Mom's waist.

We walked on each side of Mom toward the exit as she wrapped her arms around our waists. "I'm so proud of you and Denise. You both are doing extremely well. Maybe the two of you can speak to the teen group next week and give them some information to help inspire them to want to achieve."

"All right. I'll get the information from Denise."

"Hello, Pastor," I greeted as we approached. "What a wonderful sermon. I learned so much about God's expectations of us." I reached out and grabbed his hand and he gripped mine tightly.

"Good for you, Sister Reese. I hope you have thought more about working with the teens."

"Pastor, we will have to talk about that later. I'd like you to meet my best friend who is visiting with us today. This is Diana Cartwright, I said as I turned and look back at my friend."

"Welcome, Sister Cartwright. We hope that your stay was a good one and that you will return."

Shaking his hand, she smiled a beautiful smile. "Thank you! I truly enjoyed myself and I plan to come back."

Pastor shook her hand, but he could not take his eyes off me. "Have a great day, Sister Cartwright."

"Pastor, I will talk to you later," I said to remind him that we would be speaking later.

"Thank you. Please call anytime."

Diana and I stood in front of the church talking to members who invited her to come back to our church. Most of the people were friendly in the church, but as most churches did, we had our share of problem members. Trisha and the Piss Patrol walked over to where we were standing. Trisha said, "Denise, why do you think you are better than others?"

I kept talking to Diana and ignored Trisha.

"Denise, I know you hear me." She emphasized her words by using rapid hand movements. "I was just wondering why you are so fake. I see that when you come to church you are so snotty, but when you are by yourself you are friendly."

"I'm sorry, Trisha, that you have that impression of me." I smiled at her.

"I have it because that's what you show." Her group egged her on.

"Sorry." I proceeded to walk away, but she snatched my hand.

Swinging my body quickly around, I said, "Please don't touch me again."

"Or what?"

Pulling my friend close to me, I said, "Come on, Diana. Let's walk away from this. I'm not stooping that low. Sorry, you won't have me acting crazy out here."

The Pastor rushed over to me. "Sister Reese, is everything all right?"

"Yes, Pastor. I think Trisha and her friends really need your counsel."

"Trisha?"

"Yes, Pastor, I would like to schedule Bible study," Trisha said, smiling at him.

"What about the rest of you?"

"Okay," they all answered in unison. It sounded like the Piss Patrol was harmonizing.

"Thanks, Pastor. I'll talk to you later." I looked at Trisha and smiled. She shook her head. She was blessed that I didn't get crazy with her. I had enough problems trying to get my heart unlocked from the jam it was in. I didn't need other problems.

"Girl, do you have to deal with that mess often?" Diana asked incredulously.

"Only since Sister Clay spread the rumor that the pastor was interested in me. Since she did that more so-called Christians are rolling their eyes at me like I am a piece of dough and they are the dough roller."

Diana cracked up laughing. "You silly, girl."

"You have to be silly to deal with this crap. But I can

handle it. Let's go have dinner at Mom's before you go back across the water to St. Louis. I have to go to the business meeting tonight. I want to see what's going to happen."

"What do you mean what is going to happen?"

"Nothing much, we'll talk about it later."

Chapter 12

The sun set at 8:45 P. M. The business meeting was expected to start in a few minutes. Since we did not handle business on the Sabbath it was necessary to wait until the sun set. The members of the church moved slowly through the building. They were smiling and shaking hands. There were others who were hugging and talking loudly. Still, others walked in looking grumpy and angry. Thick frowns were etched across their faces, hands tucked deep inside their pockets, others with hands and arms crossed over their chests like they were trying to keep others out of their lives. I could tell by their body language they were ready to battle. They were silent and walking closely to the front of the church. As the church began to fill to capacity, I could hear voices begin to rise and I even heard a sister say, "I have a lot to say and it's not pleasant."

The pastor walked in. The church was almost as packed as service. The pastor started to address the members. "Church, please bow your heads for prayer. Father, we come to You today to ask that You will bless us as we discuss church business. Watch over this congregation tonight, Lord, and help us to conduct the business of the church as Christians. You know our needs and it is You who guides and leads us through trouble, temptation and pain. Please, God, bless us and help us to complete the task of making Your sanctuary a beautiful place to worship and congregate in. We pray. Amen."

The congregation said, "Amen."

"Church, as you know, we have been discussing the leaking roof in this sanctuary. It is not a big problem, but without attention, it is headed that way. Elder Bryant was so kind to seek three bids on the roof. If I can have your attention, he can go over the bids now. You all have the agenda for tonight. I know it has been a long day, so we will do our best to get out of this meeting soon. Elder Bryant, please come to the front."

"Pastor Davis," Brother Johnson said, standing up to do battle. "I think it is asinine to bring this up at this time. It's only June and we have more pressing problems."

"Brother Johnson," Elder Bryant said, "it is best that we handle this problem. We've had a lot of rain and with the heaviness of it beating on the roof; it is making a simple problem worse."

"But I don't think it is a problem we need to address now."

Brother Smith was ready to stop the nonsense that had been occurring in the meetings. He stood to ask a question in response to Brother Johnson's complaint.

"When is a better time, Brother Johnson? You want to wait until the roof caves in. I think what you are saying is irresponsible and stupid."

"Brother Smith, it is not necessary to speak to Brother Johnson that way. Let's conduct this meeting in an orderly and respectful manner."

"Well, Pastor, you know Brother Johnson can't do that."

"Brother Smith, I don't have a problem with you, but should you continue to talk negative about me, I will."

"Order, please. We are here to handle the roof problem. Please allow Elder Bryant to go over the bids with the church body." The pastor was trying to remain calm.

Elder Bryant distributed copies of the bid to the church. Trisha jumped up to help him pass them out on the left side of the sanctuary. She was wearing a blue denim mini skirt, and blue mules that appeared as if they had seen better days. The heels of her shoes were leaning to one side and they were too big. I could see almost two inches minus feet in the back. She had a pleasant look on her face and she was smiling. She was a pretty girl. I couldn't tell how her hair looked because it was gelled super hard into a tall upsweep and she had orange and blonde streaks going through it. But still, I sensed that with prayer her attitude would change and she would become an asset to the church.

"Church, I have received these three bids from reputable companies. As you can see on page one where I have the documented information from the Better Business Bureau for each of the companies that I received a bid on; they are in good standing, having never received complaints. I also went out and checked the roof of several churches that each repaired or re-roofed."

"Cut to the chase, Elder, what do you propose we do as a church," asked Sister Minnie Turner.

"I suggest that we go with bid three. It is with Edgemont Roofing Company; they came in with a lower bid, plus what I like most is they are in the city. I saw their work on three churches in the city and the pastors were satisfied. Plus, I do believe that if we ask our church members to support African-American businesses, we need to do it ourselves."

"Elder, I'm not worrying about who we support, I'm worrying about if we need a roof. You all have a big problem with spending the church's money on things we don't need."

"Brother Johnson, the church has not spent any money without the approval of the church board and the members," Sister Baxter said with an angry look on her face. Her mouth was twisted and her brow furrowed. "If you need to see my records I have them here with me."

"I don't need to see your records about money. You all spend a lot of time wasting it."

"Sit down," Sister Smith said while tossing her hand to Brother Johnson, "'Cause you ain't got a positive thing to say." Members in the congregation laughed, one member turned and laughed directly in Brother Johnson's face. That seemed to infuriate him more.

"Church, if we are going to complete the business of the church, we have to respect each other. We have several more areas of concern to discuss." Pastor Davis looked tired. There were lines and wrinkles across his forehead. He looked beat. His body lacked its normal energy level and he wasn't quick with his words as he had been before. He seemed sad.

"Forgive me, Pastor, but I have to say this." Sister Turner stood up. "It is so hard to do business here. There are too many cliques and angry people. For God to have delivered us from problems and pain, illnesses and so many other problems, you all seem so bitter and angry. You just don't come into the House of the Lord acting like you don't have any sense. You need to respect the pastor. He's a good, honorable man."

"I'm not too sure about honorable; I heard the pastor is having an affair with one of the sisters' daughter. This gal ain't even a Christian. So what does that say about the high and mighty pastor?"

"Brother Johnson, please don't start that rumor. You ought to be better than that." Elder Bryant was angry, he turned to walk toward Brother Johnson, but his wife snatched him back by violently pulling his jacket.

"You don't have to defend me, Elder. My business is my business. I answer to God about my private affairs."

Trisha stood up tugging on her little skirt, trying to pull it down. It had risen up so high I could see the blackness of her butt cheeks. "But you answer to us too and people are spreading rumors about you."

"You are right, Trisha. I am responsible for living up to God's expectations. So let me be clear. I am not married and should I choose to date anyone, I'll take it up with God. But the rumor you are hearing is not true."

Trisha's smile crossed her face like the boat that crossed Jordan's River. "Thank God."

"Now let's get back to the bids. I do believe we should support Edgemont Roofing. The price is right and the reputation meets all our expectations. I think we should take a vote. Could someone please make a motion?" The pastor seemed a little frustrated that he had to respond to a question so personal. He stuffed his hands into his pants pocket and rocked from side to side.

"I make a motion that we accept the bid of Edgemont Roofing because they have the lowest bid and best reputation to repair our church roof." Elder Grant turned to face the audience, since he was sitting close to the front of the church.

"Second," said Sister Cruise.

"All those in agreement with the motion say aye."

The congregation said, "Aye."

"The motion is carried," said the pastor. "The next item up for discussion is the church computers. We need to purchase new computers and renew the copier machine's agreement."

Before the pastor could finish, Brother Johnson jumped up again. "Pastor, the roof is going to cost fifteen thousand to get repaired. I realize that the congregation voted on that, but where is all this money coming from? I think we are spending money we just don't have. I still say that you and some of your cronies are mishandling the church funds. I used to be back there and since you all stopped me from working in the treasury room, now all of a sudden you all are trying to spend all our funds."

"Brother Johnson, unless you show the church where money has been misappropriated, I would appreciate it if you would be very careful how you convey your words."

"Pastor Davis. This is not a rumor. We just bought a new air conditioner that I did not agree with and the church was already being cooled with central air. So that was a stupid purchase."

Elder Bryant interrupted, "Brother Johnson, please sit down. You are trying to cause problems in the church and that is not Christ-like."

"'Cause I am honest with my words you say that is not Christ-like? Well, it's not Christ-like to steal from the church coffers."

"Please, members, may I speak?" I stood up. I don't know what led me to, but I was tired. I wanted to come back to the church, but all this arguing was a bit too much. Plus, I didn't like the way the pastor was being treated. It was so disrespectful to me. "Pastor and church members, hi, my name is Denise and I was baptized into this church's membership in my early teens. I have been away from the church for too long and I am working to return. But I am a baby in this walk with Christ and you all are making it difficult for me. I have never seen so much arguing in a church before. Is this normal? I don't want my walk with Christ to be jeopardized. We have to respect each other and be mindful of how folks see you and that includes the children, me as well as visitors who may be in our midst."

"That's right, Sister," said Sister Baxter who was standing and clapping. "Yes! That is right!"

Not a soul said anything. The pastor, who I think forgot where he was, just stared into the audience. Then our eyes met and he smiled. For a minute I saw peace float across his face. The corners of his mouth lifted up as if it was smiling to the sky. I smiled back.

"Thank you, Sister Reese. We will have to be mindful of our actions. It is important that people understand that every day we live will be a struggle in our walk with Christ, but we will pray that our actions will not hurt those people we seek to invite to walk with us. Thank you. It has been a long night. I think we should table the computers until the next meeting."

"I motion that we table the purchase of computers and the copy machine agreement until the next church business meeting," my mother said.

"I second that," said Trisha.

"Mom, why is Trisha here anyway?" I whispered into her ear. "I thought business meetings were only for board and church members."

"She decided to get baptized next month. She requested to attend, stating that she has been visiting for more than five months and she knew everything that was going on anyway. The board approved it. If she can handle this stuff she will be a better Christian for it."

"The motion can only be made by a member," shouted Brother Johnson. Trisha sat down. "I second that," Brother Johnson said with a look of satisfaction.

While the pastor prayed I tried to keep my mind on his prayer, but I kept thinking about my life. I had done something pretty awful. I had sinned and it didn't feel good. I mean, it felt good while it was happening, but the guilt was almost unbearable. I prayed that God would help guide my life and help me to stop sinning. I decided that I was going to stop seeing Darren.

I kissed Mom on the cheek and prepared to walk to the car. As I turned toward the parking lot Pastor Davis caught up to me. "Sister Reese, thanks for coming out tonight. I hope that we don't run you off. Sometimes the board meetings can get out of hand, but these are people who really care about the church."

"I understand, Pastor. I have a question to ask you."

"Whatever I can help you with I will."

"Some of the members have made comments about me to my face. Are the rumors circulating about me and you? I'm new here; I mean, I went here more than five years ago and most of these members are new to me, but basically, they don't know me."

"Let's just say that it's not just you. I have been linked to many of the women here. That comes with the job of being a minister, but one who does not have a wife brings more than speculation, it brings rumors and innuendos too."

"Does that bother you?"

"Being linked with you, no, Sister Reese. As long as the rumors do not prevent me from doing the work of God, they don't bother me. Some may slow me down, but when that happens, I pray for guidance."

"Thanks, Pastor." I got into the car and the pastor stooped down beside my car.

"Sister Reese, would you like to have dinner sometime?"

"As a friend and as my pastor, yes, I wouldn't mind that."

"That's all I ask. I'll get back to you, but plan for next Sunday."

"I will. See you later."

I pulled out of the parking lot with a laugh spreading in my heart. My heart was smiling. I could feel it. But I knew in my heart that I was too tainted to be a minister's lady. Still though, my heart smiled.

Chapter 13

As I pulled onto my street I saw flashing red lights. I wondered what was happening. I drove halfway down the street before I realized that a policeman was in front of my house, walking toward the porch.

I pulled into the driveway and an officer approached me. "Ma'am, is this your home?"

"Yes, Officer, what happened?" I jumped out of my car.

"Your neighbor called in and said that she saw a white car pull into your driveway and the passenger threw bricks through your front windows. Four windows are broken, which also caused your alarm to go off. Do you know someone who would do this?"

"No, I don't." I flung my arms down in frustration.

"Do you have any enemies?" the officer asked while peering over his eye glasses.

"No, not to my knowledge, did you say a white car?"

"Yes. Your neighbor, Ms. Brandon, said the car was a four-door white Camry. Do you know someone who drives a car like that?"

"No, but a few nights ago I spotted a white car following me and I drove to the police station and a policeman escorted me home."

"Do you remember the officer's name that escorted you home?"

"No."

"If you remember anything that can help us get to the bottom of this please call the station at this number and ask for me, Officer Peterson." He handed me a card with his number on it. "You will have to call someone to board up your windows. I can stay until they arrive and complete the job."

"Thanks, Officer."

While the windows were being boarded up, I called Diana and explained to her what had happened. She said I was welcomed to spend the night with her and I agreed. After the police officer and the glass company's worker left, I got in the car to drive off. My cell rang as I started backing out. "Hello?"

"Hey, lady, what are you up to?" Darren asked?

"Nothing."

"What's wrong? You sound sad."

I started to cry hard, fast flowing tears were running down my face and obscuring my view as I drove. "Nothing, except some maniac broke out all my windows in the front of my house."

"What?"

"You heard me. Do you think your wife knows where I live?"

"I don't think so. She wouldn't do anything like that. Jill is a great lady."

"Well, who else would be calling me and would do this?"

"I don't know. Are you staying in the house tonight?"

"No way. I am on my way to Diana's."

"What time will you get there? I will meet you."

"You stay away from me. It's over!"

"You are clearly upset and tomorrow you will see things clearer." He sighed. "I'll call you tomorrow."

"I mean it. Don't call me ever again!"

"As much as I have invested in you, I know you don't think you can walk away from me that easily without a fight." I ended the call.

Once at Diana's I explained everything to her as much as I could. As usual she blamed my relationship with Darren on all my misfortunes. She advised me to stop seeing him and pray for guidance. I agreed.

I took out my night clothes and went to soak in a warm bath. Sitting in the bubbles and drinking a tall glass of orange juice while relaxing made me feel calm. This gave me a chance to look at my life. I was not satisfied with what I saw. I was a good person who never gave my parents any real problems. I had helped others as much as I could. I had even served the poor and the homeless and ten percent of my income had always been given to charities. With all the things that I had done, I was hurt that I was going through so much. I remembered my mother used to say that when people are suffering they are going through a season. I never understood that before as I did now. I was going through something I never thought was possible. My love life was a disaster. I was sinning in that area, breaking God's laws when I should've been fearful of doing such a thing. I was being threatened by Lord knows who, even to the point of receiving prank calls and having my windows broken. I was being scorned and talked about at a church that I used to adore when I was a teenager. I was going through a season of pain, problems and my own hell; one that I had been the main contributor to.

I wanted to change. It was time for me to live my life according to God's will. I knew that letting go of a man that I loved so much was going to be painful and difficult. But I had also been told that there were no burdens that God wouldn't help me through. So I would change for the better.

I laid my head back on the pillow in the Jacuzzi and continued to think. *I love me too much to suffer like this. I love me too much to be hurt over a man. I am sure that this is the doing of his wife. I am not willing to fight for a man who was never mine from the start.*

I whispered, "Lord, please help me to change. Save me from sin. Give me the courage to leave Darren and help me to become more like Jesus. I don't want to be lost, God. I don't want to break any of Your commandments. I want to love You and do Your will. Strengthen and protect me from danger. Protect me from those that seek to hurt and destroy me, but most of all, God forgive me for my sins. Amen."

I laid back and allowed the tears to flow. My tears were many and silent. My cries were internal; my heart was tied into knots. I was releasing the hurt, the bad, the sad, and the sin that threatened to destroy me.

Diana pounded on the door. "Are you okay in there?" She opened the door and walked in.

Lifting my body up to give her eye contact, "Yes, Diana, I'm fine."

"If you need me, just holler and I will be right there." She folded her hands up.

I laid my head back down. "I know. Thank you so much for your help."

Backing out of the room, she smiled, showing her beautiful white teeth. "No problem." She backed out of the door and closed it.

Chapter 14

I woke up at eight o'clock Sunday morning. My eyes were so swollen from crying, yet I couldn't think of myself. I called mother and asked if she had spoken to Cynthia, Sarah's daughter.

"No, she has not returned my calls. That is surprising. She always called me back."

"Well, it is possible she is out of town. But still, if she knew that her mother's best friend was calling you would think she would return the call to make sure nothing is wrong with her mother."

"Well, all kids are not like you. I'm blessed to have a child like you." I could almost feel mother's smile coming through the phone.

"Thanks, Mother. Is everything else okay?"

"Yes. Everything is fine."

"Call me if you hear from Cynthia. I'll talk to you later, okay?"

"Okay. Bye now."

"Bye, Mom."

I jumped out of bed, showered and put my clothes on. I decided to see if Diana was out of bed, but as I walked toward her bedroom I heard her moving things around in the kitchen. "Good morning, Diana."

"Good morning, Denise. Did you sleep well?"

"Yes, I did. Thank you so much for letting me stay," I said as I hugged her close.

"You know you are always welcome here. I hate seeing you go through so much. You are such a good person."

"Diana, I love you and I appreciate you being in my life, but please don't start that 'you are a good girl' stuff with me, because if that was true I wouldn't be with Darren." I walked over to the kitchen walnut-wooded cabinets, grabbed a coffee cup and poured me a cup of coffee.

"When did you start drinking coffee?"

"I really don't drink it. Every now and then I drink a cappuccino and since you don't have that and I don't feel like going to pick up a cup, this will do fine." I stood there sipping my coffee and listening to my friend.

"What do you plan to do today?"

"I'm going back home. I can't hide out here forever." I put down my cup and pulled out the chair from the table to sit down.

"Well, you should since you don't know who did it. People are crazy and you can't put anything past them."

I picked up my coffee and to cool it down I blew air on the

dark brown liquid. "I know, but I'm not scared because I haven't hurt anyone, so no one has the right to hurt me, or the reason."

"What if it is his wife?" Diana stood up and poured herself a second cup.

"If it is then she is seriously ill." I stared off into space. Diana, you have always been in my corner even though I do the one thing with Darren that you despise. Why aren't you angry with me?"

Sitting back down at the table, she said, "I lost my husband to a woman like you."

Peering over my coffee mug, I asked, "What do you mean a woman like me?"

"You know, a woman who unknowingly dates a married man, but stays even after she finds out the truth. I know that my husband started it, got involved, made the woman want him, but still I blamed them both. I'm not angry at you because I understand the loneliness, the headache and the massive amounts of love that the mistress has for the married man. I just wish that once the woman finds out she leaves and never enters a relationship like that again. But I know that things like this will always happen."

"You are such a good person. I am sorry that this happened to you."

"Thank you, but God had my back. You know the Bible says that he who finds a wife finds a good thing; my ex-husband lost someone who was a good thang, that's all. I should go to the house with you."

"That's okay. I'll be all right." I suddenly heard my cell phone muffled ringing. "Is that my cell ringing? What did I do with my purse?" I stood up and pushed the chair back to search for my phone. I walked toward the living room with Diana on my heels.

"There it is on the couch." Diana pointed in the direction of the ringing.

I picked up the phone, and then hit send before it stopped ringing. "Hello? No, I can't see you today. Let it go. It's over." I pushed the word end so hard on the cell I broke my nail.

"Wow, you are serious, aren't you?" Diana moved closer and grabbed my hand. "You broke your nail. Does that hurt?"

"No, it didn't break at the nail bed. I have to be serious. I'm not about this drama and once I let him go his wife will stop harassing me."

"Good for you."

"Tell you what, I am going to drive over to see Sarah and take her out to breakfast."

"You are really worried about her, aren't you?"

"Yes. Now I can see why she has been drinking. Her daughter still hasn't returned Mom's call. She must know it is about her mother. Maybe Sarah's lonely, which is a major reason that senior citizens drink."

"That's so sad. Girl, don't let that happen to me."

"I won't because we will be old and still kicking it. I'll call you later."

I looked at my watch as I drove across the bridge. I arrived in thirty-five minutes to Sarah's house. Walking up to her door, grasping the brochures in one hand, I knocked hard with my free one. I continued to knock for five minutes. When Sarah came to the door, it was very obvious that she had been drinking.

"Hi, Sarah. I came by to see how you are doing."

"Come have a drink with meeee."

I looked at Sarah; her eyes were blood shot and she was stumbling up toward her living room like she was walking up stairs. I ran behind her and helped her to the living room.

"Let me go. I can make it. I just had one drank!"

I walked over and picked up an almost-empty bottle of E & J. I was worried and knew that I would have to intervene in some way. I needed to talk to her daughter soon.

"When was the last time you talked to Cynthia?"

"Cynthia? The last time she needed money. She calls every now and then and that ain't enough, considering I'm her mother."

"Have you told her you miss her?"

"What for? All she gonna say is I'll be there in a couple of months, then something comes up."

"Why don't you visit her?"

"She said the same thing. But I don't want to be a bother."

"Sarah, I am worried about you. It is so easy to overindulge and get into trouble. Oftentimes, you won't even know that you are overdoing it."

"I only drink to ease my loneliness."

"I know. But I think it would be a good idea to attend a meeting. You can talk about it with someone who can help. I could go with you as the family member on the first visit to a treatment program or to an Alcoholics Anonymous meeting." I tried looking her in the face, but she continued to avoid my glance. Remembering the brochures that I had brought for her, I handed them to her.

"Just take these and read them when you get a chance. We can talk later. Have you eaten anything?" I walked to the kitchen, opened the refrigerator and then pulled out eggs, turkey bacon, butter and cheese. "Sarah, I'm going to hook us up a nice breakfast, okay?"

"Do what you want!" She belligerently yelled.

Oooooh, that was loud. She can't hear herself screaming. Now that's drunk.

It didn't take long to cook our breakfast. I prepared our

plates and walked in to get Sarah. She was sitting in her chair, staring at the wall. I walked over and pulled her out of the chair and hugged her. She kissed my cheek.

"You are such a sweet girl."

"Thank you."

I slipped my arm around her tiny waist and walked into the kitchen with her. She put her drink down and sat at the table. She looked sad. I sat her plate down in front of her and coaxed her to eat. She ate all of it. We talked about everything, but it was clear, she was lonely. I decided to talk to her daughter and check with the pastor to see what kind of activities they could find for her and whether the church had an activity bus. I thought that would help.

"Stay with me tonight, Denise."

I hesitated, but rationalized that she was my mother's best friend and she needed help. If I stayed, maybe she wouldn't drink. I decided to stay because she needed me and the longer I stayed away from Darren the stronger I would become in letting him go for good.

I called mother and she joined us and brought me a change of clothing. We sat on the floor and ate finger foods that Momma brought over. We laughed and talked way into the midnight hour. Sarah did not drink anything else that day. I knew she would need an intervention, support group, and all the encouragement to stop. I was prepared to help her. Helping her helped me deal with my own loneliness and letting go of my problems.

I tried never to have meetings at work on Mondays, so I knew that I could stay with Sarah and try to help her without a disruption in my assignments that I planned to complete at work. Around seven o'clock Monday morning, I called my secretary to alert her of my taking a personal day, and after discussing a few issues with her, I went back to bed. When I woke up Sarah was talking to Cynthia. It was almost ten o'clock. I had slept most of the morning away. Mother informed me that she had spoken to Cynthia. Cynthia decided to take a couple of weeks off to come see about her mother. She would arrive in seven days.

Chapter 15

Pulling up into my driveway, I shuddered. It was almost two in the afternoon. Darren pulled in behind me. I jumped out of the car and walked into the house. He pulled his car in next to mine in the garage and walked in, grabbed the remote and closed the garage and kitchen door.

"Denise!" He screamed my name loud and harsh.

I turned and walked back into the kitchen. "Why are you here?"

"I came to check on you. I see you got the windows fixed. That was fast."

"Yes, it was. They did it earlier today. My neighbor let them in."

"Do you know who did it?"

"Your wife."

"I told you she would never do anything like that and I meant it."

"You don't know what a person would do when they are hurting?"

"She doesn't know where you live!"

"That's what you think. Women know when their men are seeing someone else and they can find out anything. By the way, what happened to your so-called divorce?"

"It's still on."

"So what did you tell her you were divorcing her for, irreconcilable differences or what?"

"What's gotten into you?" Darren was so angry that before I knew it he had grabbed my arm.

"Let my arm go! You're hurting me, Darren!"

"Stop acting a fool before I do more than hurt you." He pushed me toward the bedroom, I tripped and he jerked me up.

"Please leave. Get out!"

Slap! His hand connecting to my face sounded like a ball slamming against a door. The pain felt like I had been hit with a bottle. Grabbing my face to quiet the pain, I screamed, "Oh, God, I can't believe you hit me! Get out before I call the police!" I felt so humiliated. My heart was beating rapidly and I felt as if I would faint. I couldn't believe he hit me.

As I stood there rubbing the part of my face that he hit, I looked into his eyes. I saw so much anger. Then I noticed that he started unbuttoning his shirt. "Why are you undressing?"

"You made me angry and I need to release the stress."

I turned, ran toward the door and he snatched me back

into his arms. He kissed me and tried to put his tongue in my mouth. When I wouldn't let him he hit me again. He snatched my blouse off, and threw me onto the bed and stripped me naked.

"Please don't rape me," I begged between sobs.

"I'm not raping you." He ripped my underwear off and entered me forcefully. "I'm making love to my fiancée."

He moaned and grunted so loudly while I cried and asked God to help me. He raped me for more than an hour, taking me twice. My lip bled and there was blood on his mouth where he tried to kiss me. When it was over, he turned over on his back. I was exhausted from trying to fight him off of me.

"Go cook me something."

I looked at him like he had lost his mind. It felt as if smoke was coming out of every hole in my body. He was a stranger. This was not the man I knew. He hissed at me. Then he jumped up in my face.

"Do you think I have ruined my marriage to be told that it's over? It's over when I say it is. Don't make me hurt you. I told my wife I wanted a divorce and broke her heart and you think it is going to be easy? This is my life you are playing with."

I flinched. I knew not to say anything to make him angrier, so I backed up and walked into the kitchen. I cooked his dinner while he watched my every move.

"I love you."

I didn't respond.

"I said I love you."

I turned to say something, but when I jerked around he was in my face, kissing me and whispering he didn't mean to hurt me. He lifted me into his arms and carried me back to the bedroom. We made love. I held onto him because I loved him. I held onto him because I believed he loved me too. I held onto him because I was scared not to. I held on so that I wouldn't be lonely and sitting at home drinking like Sarah. He wouldn't let me go.

After dinner, we cuddled and watched a movie. The phone rang, but I refused to answer. The number of the person calling was blocked. After five times, I picked up the phone.

"I have had it with you," the caller hissed as if their mouth was closed and they were speaking through their teeth. "I told you that I was going to hurt you. I guess breaking your windows was not enough? I see I am going to have to break your arm."

"Who is this?"

Darren grabbed the phone. "Don't call this number again or you will have to deal with me!" He looked at the phone's mouthpiece as if he could see the person. "Whoever it was hung up."

"Is it your wife, Darren?"

"Jill would not call here. She left to go stay with her mother in Florida. She asked me not to break up our family over a fling. I told her that it was not because of another woman. I was unhappy."

"You really don't think she knows where I live?"

"Honestly, I don't think she knows. Do you have someone else who is angry with you?"

"No, I don't. Well, there is one person, but she doesn't know anything about me."

"That's who we need to look at."

"I'll do some checking in the morning. Darren, don't ever put your hands on me again or I can't promise what I will do."

"I'm sorry. I just don't want to lose you. You mean so much to me. I can stay all week with you, and when Jill returns we can discuss other stuff later."

I stood there like an idiot, smiling. What is wrong with me? I walked into my guest bedroom and pretended to be looking for something, but I cried and asked God to forgive me. *How many times will God forgive me for the same sin?*

Chapter 16

The first thing I did, even before Darren woke up, was call Sister Clay. We had not spoken since that day at the barbeque, but I could feel she was up to something. I tried to think about when the calls first started. Was it before or after the barbeque or that little incident at church or the phone call? I couldn't think. *Would she be so bold as to break out my windows?*

I picked up the phone and dialed her number. The phone rang five times before she answered. "Hi, Sister Clay."

Sounding so peaceful and friendly in her go-to-church voice, she asked, "Denise, is that you?"

"Yes. It is and I have a question to ask you," I said as I swung my legs over the arm of the couch.

"What, dear? What can I help you with?"

"Have you been calling and hanging up on me?"

"What? You must be kidding!" she said with attitude coming from the phone, no longer the sweet voice, but that of an angry bull. "You know, I am going to speak to Pastor Davis about you. What is wrong with you? Are you accusing me of something? You know the pastor needs to check out folks before he starts dating them."

"For your information and I am saying this to you one last time, I am not dating the pastor and if I were it is not your business."

"Oh my, you are such an angry person. I wouldn't have ever thought you were like this. Your mother must be disappointed in your attitude. You don't call me and disrespect me. You need to be put into check, young girl."

"Excuse me, but you have been spreading rumors about me and trying to get all in my business ever since I stepped on that church parking lot."

"How dare you? I am reporting this to the pastor and if he doesn't take action I will be contacting the church board to register a complaint against you."

"And while you are at it, tell them you owe me fifteen hundred dollars for breaking out my front windows." I heard a loud click. *I know she didn't hang that phone up on me.*

I sat back down on the couch, too mad to think. I had to say a quick prayer. "Lord, the devil is on my back, please help me." I could hear Darren taking a shower. The nerve of Sister Clay, I knew she was the one calling me. "What kind of car does she drive anyway?"

When the shower stopped, I went into the bathroom and turned the water back on in the shower and seduced Darren again. My love for Darren was stronger than ever. Spending the entire night with me showed me how good it would be with him. I would definitely have to figure out another way to receive atonement for my sins. I was going to marry Darren, so I wasn't sinning, now was I?

****

It was a long day at work. Mother called to let me know that Cynthia would be arriving the following Sunday. It was the quickest she could get leave from work. I would have to make sure that I had all my resources together and other information on alcoholism and the elderly so that Cynthia would be well-informed.

I had to attend a community health networking meeting in East St. Louis. I was a part of a new coalition that was focusing on the healthcare needs of children and the elderly. Our primary goal was to help reduce and eliminate the high rate of infant mortality in the metropolitan area, which included St. Louis, Missouri, Centreville, Illinois, Cahokia, East St. Louis and fifteen other municipalities. After the meeting I decided to check on Mother and then Sarah.

I arrived at Mother's around noon; she and I had lunch together. Mother fixed us a chef salad with crabmeat, turkey, ham, raisins, seasoned almonds, purple onions, Romaine and Iceberg lettuce. We chatted about everything.

"Denise, Sister Clay would not break out your windows. Didn't you say that Darren's wife was angry at him for asking for a divorce?"

"Yeah, but he swears she would never do anything like that. He claims that she doesn't even know where I live."

"You know, Denise, when you play with fire you are going to soon get burned. You were wrong. Darren has the characteristics of a man who cheats. He came over to meet the family once and he was elusive when I asked him questions. Plus, sweetheart, he had a tan on his ring finger. That is why I chose not to say anything to you when you came over after you found out. You were already hurting."

"I asked him about that tan, but he said it came from wearing a ring his dad gave him."

"Your sister told me the week before you found out that she heard he was married."

"Terri is something else. I wish she would have told me, but then again I wouldn't have believed her."

"She didn't tell anyone but me."

"Was she mad at me?"

"No, she was just shocked that you would date a married man. Plus, she saw him with her on her campus last week and said they looked quite chummy."

"She was sadly mistaken. His wife is in Florida, waiting on him to change his mind about the divorce."

"Sweetheart, you need to step aside and let them work out their problems. You and Darren are committing a sin and if you all stop and ask God to forgive you, He will. But what you are doing is wrong. The Bible says that marriage is sacred and that no man should put it asunder. Do you understand that?"

"I didn't know that he was married when I started seeing him. I found out two years later and by that time I was too involved. My heart was deeply connected to him."

"It doesn't matter. Just because he lied to you should tell you about his character. A man who lies and cheats with one wife is guaranteed to do it with the next one. Every time he is not with you, he'll be accused of having an affair. You will not trust him because you've helped teach him how to mislead and lie to his wife."

"Don't blame me. He did that all by himself."

"No, Denise, you helped to create him because you allowed it to continue once you found out."

"I love him and I want him. Why can't I be with the man I love without the guilt and shame?"

"Because he is not yours."

I held my head down, afraid for Mom to see the pain buried deep inside my eyes. When I left her house I still wouldn't allow my eyes to meet hers. I left feeling dejected.

I drove from Mom's house to Sarah's. I decided that since I was in the area I would visit her before I left. As I pulled into her driveway I noticed that her car was there, but I still had an eerie feeling. I went up to her porch and proceeded to knock on the door and that was when I noticed the smell and next I saw the smoke.

"Sarah! Sarah! Can you hear me? Open the door!" I banged on the door. I grabbed the door knob, but the heat from the fire scorched my hand. "Ouch, ouch, my hand!" Even though my hand was in immeasurable pain, I kept banging and then started kicking the door.

I looked toward the back of the house and saw gray, thick smoke billowing out the kitchen window. I turned and saw two men walking up. "Please help me; I think Ms. Sarah is in the house!"

"No way," one of them hollered. They kicked in the door and rushed into the house with me trailing not far behind. The larger man turned and told me to go back, it was too smoky. I did. Minutes later they brought her out of the house. They sat her on the grass far away from the house.

"Are you okay, Sarah?" I reached down to kiss her cheek and when I did I smelled liquor, and it was strong. *Oh, my God!*

The fire was contained to the kitchen, which was close to the front of the house. Someone had called the fire department and an ambulance. The ambulance took Sarah to the hospital and I had Mom to meet her there. I wanted to stay and secure her house. I called Cynthia on my cell to tell her what had happened. She was upset and afraid for her mother.

"Is my mom okay?"

"Yes. They wanted to check her out, she kept coughing and they wanted to help clear her lungs from the effects of the smoke."

"How did the fire start?"

Sitting down and crossing my legs on the brick wall in front of the house, I responded, "I don't know, Cynthia. But truthfully, I smelled liquor on her. It seemed to me that she had been drinking, and heavily this time."

"This drinking thing is serious. Did you talk to her?" Cynthia hesitated for a second as if she was trying to sort this out in her mind.

"No, I just smelled it on her."

"If you can handle things for me I will try to get there on a late flight. I appreciate what you are doing for Mom."

I stood up and paced back and forth on the concrete. I let out a huge breath. "She's like my mom, too."

"I know. She has always been crazy about you. Thanks, Denise. I'll call you when I get settled there." She hung up the phone.

I stayed and got Sarah's home boarded up to prevent folks from breaking in. The home reeked of smoke and soot. Water dripped out of the kitchen curtains, and piled in puddles throughout the kitchen and hallway. In addition, there was ash and grime attached to everything in the house. Though the kitchen was not burned badly, smoke damage was prevalent throughout the entire house and it needed to be boarded up until Cynthia arrived to handle the insurance, and her mother. By the time I got home late that evening I was so tired. I dragged myself through the door and took off my clothes. I tossed my shoes into the corner and threw my shirt and skirt on my treadmill. I grabbed my XX L T-shirt, poured me a glass of cold tea and dropped on the couch in the den. Darren was set to arrive around seven with Chinese food. I grabbed the book, *A Fresh Encounter* from my coffee table. It was written by Ann Clay, who wrote romance novels and inspirational books. I needed something positive in my life, so I began reading it.

I Surrender All

A surrendered life is a transformed life, and it affects everything we do and everyone who touches us. Surrendered lives have order. They know how and when to give praise, how and when to worship, and when to submit to others.

Submit to others out of reverence to Christ. —Ephesians 5:21 (NIV)

Rejoice in a Time of Trouble

The suffering and pain in our lives have purpose, and it is promised that good will come from it. However, without faith, we easily fall into the trap of hopelessness, even when we wish for good things in our struggle.

To reap the benefits of our despair we must have trust that the Lord will prevail in our situations.

We often ask when will He come to our rescue? Why is this happening to us? How long must we suffer before God relieves us of our burdens? How do we handle such a task? What makes our situation so unique that we require more than what God has already given?

The answer lies in our spiritual lives. We must understand that we are not yet what God wants us to be. He still has work to do in all of us. We must trust Him unconditionally and wait patiently while He molds us into what we are to become, even if it hurts.

When our faith is unraveling, Christ brings us into the highest places, where we are privileged to enjoy His glory. And we rejoice when we are blessed enough to experience those occasions. In the same way, we should rejoice when we run into trials and tribulations, for we know that they, too, are good for us.

Trouble builds character in us, which keeps us close to God and helps strengthen our confidence in Him for our expected salvation. Expected salvation keeps us rooted and seldom disappointed, because we know how dearly God loves us. He has given us the Holy Spirit to fill our hearts with His love. At the right time, He will save us from our enemy and ourselves.

I tell you the truth you will weep and mourn while the world rejoices. You will grieve but your grief will turn to joy.

John 16:20 (NIV)

Reading always soothed my soul and that inspirational book was doing the same thing. It seemed that the section I chose to read was trying to tell me something. I was calmer and more centered. As I read the book my heart rate slowed down and my headache subsided. I also lost that feeling of anxiousness that made me want to run throughout the house until I collapsed from exhaustion. I fell asleep on the couch. I was awakened by the ringing of the doorbell. I jumped off the couch and walked to the door. I looked out my peephole, but I didn't see anyone. So I waited and then opened the door. There was a package sitting near my rocking chair and it was addressed to me. I opened it and there were two cans of dog food and a small canister of Mace. *This is weird.*

Darren arrived two hours later. I gave the package to him and he stared at it. He examined the handwriting with the skill of a surgeon. His finger slid across the writing on the package like he was trying to read Braille. Then he glowered at every inch of the box, looking for something that would enlighten him about the sender. He said I needed to call the police and reminded me that Jill was in Florida. "Jill couldn't have done this."

I rushed to the phone, picked up the receiver and dialed the police department and they arrived within twenty minutes. They took the package and observed it closely. "It's just a couple cans of dog food." The officer couldn't hold back his laughter. A smile stretched across his face and he bent his head down to camouflage how silly it was to waste his time. It was the same officer who responded to my windows being broken. This time he asked me firmly, "Do you have any enemies?"

"No!" I shouted to show my frustration.

"Ms. Reese, this is the second call to this house in less than two weeks. Are you sure you don't know who is angry at you?"

"Officer McNeil, I don't have any enemies." I'm sure he wanted to laugh again. His chest heaved. Finding two cans of dog food should've been a blessing for a dog owner, but I knew it meant more. I just felt it.

Rolling his eyes, he looked at Darren. "Are you the husband?"

"No." Darren didn't say another word.

"Well, Ms. Reese, I would think that someone is trying to give you a message and that message seems to be that you are a dog, or a b...but I won't say the word." He could barely keep from laughing. Although his mouth was closed, his chest was hiccupping, like someone trying to hold a cough in. "The mace may mean either you need to use it to protect yourself or it's going to be used on you. You will need to come to the station and complete a police report." Looking around, he said, "I take it that you reported the windows?"

"No, I didn't."

"Well, you need the report to show that you have documented these actions being taken against you." He turned and looked at Darren again. He actually stared at him like he knew that he was involved either voluntarily or involuntarily. He turned back to me. "Be careful, Ms. Reese."

I walked the policeman out the front door. Once in the yard, he said, "I know it is not my business, but you seem like a pretty nice young lady, is he married?"

"Yes, but he is divorcing her." He smiled. His eyes were bright, like a glow light and I felt like he was laughing at me. I frowned.

"I'm sorry I reacted like that. Didn't mean to insinuate that he was like most men who lie, but are you sure that this doesn't have anything to do with him?"

"No, I'm not."

"Just be careful and monitor your surroundings. People are different now; they will act on their threats."

"Thanks again."

I walked back into the house. Darren pulled me toward him and looked me in the eyes. I closed my eyes and he kissed them one at a time. Then he pulled me into his chest and said, "I won't allow anyone to hurt you. Please trust me when I say I was married for ten years and my wife is not like that."

"Pain changes people." I removed myself from his embrace and strolled into the kitchen. I prepared our dinner and we ate in silence. After dinner we removed the plates from the table and cleaned the kitchen together. Once completed, he wrapped his arms around my waist and we went into the great room to watch television. Darren fell asleep on the couch and I sat and watched him. The tears would not stop. I cried softly so that he couldn't hear me. When the tears overwhelmed me I went to the bathroom and turned the shower on and cried big gut-wrenching sobs that reached from the bottom of my feet to the top of my head. Cries that made my face scrunch up like a wrinkled old man's. Eyeliner and mascara rolled down my face like little ants forming a line to build an ant hill. I didn't trust my feelings and my intuition. I felt lost and unloved; God was teaching me a lesson and if I didn't wake up and hear Him, I would suffer greatly.

Chapter 17

I arrived at church with Diana on my side. She had called and asked me to pick her up. Diana started spending more time with me lately because she was worried about me. I was just glad that she cared. I was exhausted. Earlier during the week I informed my employees that I would take a vacation in two weeks. I desperately needed the time.

Pastor Davis was into his sermon when we arrived. He was talking about love and commitment. He challenged the congregation to fall in love with God. "If you fall in love with Him, your dreams will come true. If you fall in love with Him, you will not be afraid to live and love. He already loves you. The Bible says in John 3:16, please turn with me, *For God so loved the world that He gave His only begotten Son so that we could have everlasting life.* That's a God who cares. That's a God who loves you. He won't leave you. He won't forsake you. He won't break your heart. He is your doctor. He is your friend. He's your light in darkness. He is your brother, your mother, your friend, your lover; God is your everything and He won't break your heart. Do you know my Godddd? He's wonderful." The congregation rose to their feet, clapping, and some were dancing. I sat there with tears flooding my face. I thought it was my message. He was preaching about me.

The organist played, while the drummer began the song, "Do You Know My Jesus?" I sang and cried. "He's a friend of mine. Do you know my Jesus? He's with me all the time. He never lets me walk alone, that's why I sing this song. Do you know him?" I could barely contain my joy that God was with me and yes indeed, I knew Him.

After the service, everyone was hugging and feeling good.

I had re-introduced Diana to everyone. "I really like your church," she reminded me. "You know the pastor can really preach and teach." She kissed the side of my face.

As we moved through the line, Trisha looked at me and spoke. I spoke back. As we moved forward in the receiving line, the pastor took my hand and squeezed it. "Would you come back, Sister Reese, to work with the teens? They are having a rap session and the sister who works with them is ill, so we need a speaker."

"Pastor, your sermon today really hit me hard. Thank you. I felt like you were talking directly to me." He smiled. His teeth were beautiful. They were sparkling white and not one was out of its designated place. "What time shall I come back?"

"They will meet after the sun goes down; around eight-forty-five. Thank you. I will be here to introduce you."

He shook my hand again and welcomed Diana to our church and reminded her she was always welcomed. She smiled like a Cheshire cat. As we walked out of the church door, she whispered, "If you don't want him I do."

"Go for it, girl. Go for what you know."

"Naw, my sister, he only has eyes for you."

"Diana, I don't know why people think that, he's just a friendly pastor"

"Don't forget friendly and fine."

As we walked to the car I saw a small group gathering. "Girl, what's going on over there?"

"Diana, your guess is as good as mine; but we'll know in a minute."

When we got closer to my car I saw immediately that it was my best friend, Sister Clay, and a couple of her so-called Christian friends, walking toward me.

"Sister Clay, come on, this is the Sabbath. Don't act like this at the church," one of the church ladies said.

"I don't care where we are. She called me at home talking mess and I am getting this stuff straight today. Denise, I need to talk to you."

I know she wasn't getting ready to trip on the parking lot.

"Diana, it looks like we have company. Don't tell me I'ma have to fight."

"Denise, why did you call me with that mess? I don't 'preciate you questioning me about something so stupid. Whatever you have to say, please say it now."

I gave her a look that said I would knock the mess out of her. I rolled my eyes to the sky and balled my fists up. She backed up.

"I think it is best that you walk away from me now."

She put her hand on her hip. "So you're threatening me? You little tramp."

"I asked you, Sister Clay, to walk away from me before someone gets hurt."

The woman was pushing and acting like she was getting ready to hit me and her friends were pulling her back. I couldn't believe that forty-plus-year-old woman wanted to fight me on church grounds. I wanted to be as crazy as she was acting, but Diana had my arm and wouldn't let it go.

"Don't let me go, because I'm going to hurt her. She thinks she is better than others anyway. Wait until the pastor hears about you." Sister Clay's left hand was balled up into a fist and she was huffing and puffing like she had been running.

"I don't think you have to wait. He's already walking over and he heard everything you said."

"Pastor, Denise Reese is a troublemaker. She is a liar and she, she—"

"Sister Clay, please stop talking now."

"But, Pastor, she is dating a married man. That should tell you about her character."

The pastor whirled around to look at me. I saw a hint of disappointment in his eyes. His eyelids drooped a little, almost like a person who was experiencing a self-esteem problem. He requested that the crowd leave.

Once everyone had cleared the area and Diana had gotten into the car to wait on me, the pastor asked what was going on.

"This girl called my house, accusing me of calling her and hanging up. I don't have time for those kinds of stupid games."

"Yes, I called her. Anytime a woman constantly asks your business and spreads negative stuff about you, I figured she would call and play games on the telephone, too."

"Sister Clay, this is something that has nothing to do with the church and this shouldn't be happening here on neither the church grounds nor anywhere else. I suggest that we take this into counsel."

"Pastor, please don't waste your time. I have nothing else to say about this matter." I turned to walk to my car.

"I want to talk because she is seeing a married man. I have heard the rumors. But she sits in the church like she is holier than thou or something."

"That's enough, Sister Clay."

I quickly turned to look at Ms. Clay. I felt like smoke was billowing out of my ears. I was heated now. I looked at her and she was smiling like she had just toppled Iraq and rescued the United States military.

"Pastor, see what I mean about her gossiping and causing problems? I am twenty-five and she is over forty, yet she's acting like a teen."

I left them both standing there and jumped into my car and pulled off. I would take care of Sister Clay later.

"Dag, what's wrong with that lady?" Diana shook her head in amazement.

"She is not a Christian and if she is, I'm definitely in the wrong place."

"Do you think the pastor believes her?"

"No, I don't. But he might. Heck, everybody is talking about me. It goes with success."

****

I decided not to let the action of the day keep me from my promise to work with the teens. I arrived at the church at eight-thirty. I was still embarrassed about the pastor hearing that I was seeing a married man. Now I was sure that Sister Clay was behind the calls and my broken windows. Next, I would just have to prove it and once I did, I would press charges.

I wondered why I was so embarrassed by my actions. I wondered if I was more ashamed that the pastor and others knew about me. If that was the case, why didn't I leave Darren? How could I stand before the teens and young adults when I was suffering from low self-esteem? Even though I was successful and had the car and the house, I still let a man who was not my husband take advantage of my heart. I shook off the negative thinking, got out of the car, set my car alarm and then walked into the church.

When I walked into the fellowship hall, I saw the pastor standing at the window, looking into the courtyard. I wanted to run. I didn't want him to see me. He was in deep thought. Just as I safely passed him I heard," Hi, Denise. The youth will be meeting in the young adult room tonight."

"Thanks, Elder Bryant." As I walked away I looked back at Pastor Davis. He didn't say a word and did not even smile. *Sister Clay is right about his feelings for me. I can't believe it; a pastor is interested in me. I must be seeing things.* His eyes were sad and his lips appeared to be pointing down as if in a sad frown. *Well, at least he knows that I could never be a first lady. But I feel bad. We have dinner scheduled tomorrow. I will call him later and cancel.*

I walked into the young adult room and put down my briefcase. Once I began forming the chairs into a semi-circle, Pastor Davis walked in and helped me. We didn't say a word. When we finished organizing the room, I whispered, "Thank you, Pastor."

"You're welcome, Sister Reese." Just then the door opened and in walked twenty noisy teenagers. They were chewing and popping gum and several were blowing huge bubbles. One young man, Tim James, slung a huge book bag filled with pencils and notepads on a desk. The pastor had to settle everybody down. Tim told everyone that he had writing tools for them.

The pastor introduced me and I walked up. I asked the

group to introduce themselves. I also had each teen take a card out of my brown sack. Each would have to answer the questions they selected. I pulled one also. We discussed self-esteem issues, relationships and all sorts of teenage questions. We had a great time. To end the rap session, I read a poem.

CHRISTIAN

I'm a Christian

I'm a Christian

Can't you see?

God won't let no one

Mess with me

If I read my Bible

And pray every day

God said, He'll protect me

From day to day.

If someone tells you to do something wrong

Run, don't walk until you get away.

Another student read a poem from a Langston Hughes book. I had brought several poetry books to read from. I had planned to introduce them to poetry writing because it is an excellent way to express your feelings about different issues. A student named Karen selected the poem entitled the world.

THE WORLD

The world is a great big place

So big you can't cover it, not even in a race

Be humble, prayerful and appreciate,

And don't do anything negative or in bad taste.

One day the Lord will return and take us to a place

so beautiful,

Big, powerful and great.

It's there for each of us, if we have faith.

Be good and faithful and let's run this race

We can win it

If we keep our mind in good taste,

And our feet in a safe, blessed place.

Justine selected one called, Like You, Jesus. She read with passion. She projected her voice as if she was speaking to Jesus Himself. Her gestures were on target. She punctuated her sounds perfectly.

Like you, Jesus

Like you, Jesus, I strive to be,

Loving, faithful and compassionate, too.

Help me to always love others, in my efforts to be like you.

Teach me to pray so that I'll know what to say and do.

Walk with me through the night and protect me, too.

Help me to encourage others, as they, too, try to be like you.

When I'm feeling sad and blue and I don't know what to do.

Show me, lead me and push me, if you have to.

Lord, remember me

'Cause I'm the girl who wants to be just like YOU!

The young people really enjoyed the poems. "Who wrote those poems?" asked Tim.

"I'll let you know the next time I return."

"I like those. Very simplistic and enjoyable," Tanya said. "Maybe when you come back we can do a poetry night."

"That would be nice." I knew that would happen, that's why I wanted them to read poems.

"So when will you come back?" Tim wanted to know.

"I'm not sure, but soon," I said. I really did enjoy the teens and would've loved to work with them on their creative sides.

As we prepared to leave, I asked someone to pray. Janice volunteered. "Everybody close your eyes. Heavenly Father, we want to thank You for Your many blessings. We pray that You will bless each person that stands before You in this meeting. Bless our families and the church congregation.

We pray that You will move Denise Reese's mind to come back and possibly become a teen leader. We enjoyed her conversation and the way she allowed us to share information. Give us traveling mercies and help us to make it home safely. Amen."

"Thanks, Janice, that was beautiful."

"Will you come back to meet with us again?"

"Sure. Thanks for participating."

I hugged each teen as they left the room. The pastor returned. "I hear that everyone enjoyed you. I told you that you would make a great teen leader."

"Thanks." I started to walk out of the room, but the pastor called me back in. "Denise. Are we still on for dinner tomorrow, I'd like to talk to you about some things?"

"What time?"

"Five o'clock would be great."

"I'll see you then." Pastor walked me to my car. I thanked him, started the car and pulled off the lot.

During my drive home, I decided to call Darren. "Hi, baby." "Hey, sweetheart. I'm going to be late tonight. I'm still at the university, working with the graduate assistant, Tammy. We are trying to complete these papers before the summer session is over."

"All right. Grab a bite to eat. I'm not up to cooking."

"I've already eaten. Tammy picked up something not too long ago. So I'll see you later."

"All right, I'll see you when you get here. Bye."

I called Diana to chat. "Girl, things went well tonight. The teens asked me to come back again."

"That's good. Did you see the pastor?"

"Yes. He came to introduce me. He looked sad. He lacked good eye contact and it seemed he was having a hard time trying to smile."

"Well, considering that he is interested in you and he just found out that you are dating a married man, something he no doubt teaches his members not to do, I can understand the hurt."

"It's not like he ever approached me."

"He's the pastor. He has to be careful. He can't go around dating anybody. He has a position of authority that can't be misused or abused. He has to be careful who he chooses. To find out that you might be dating a married man, that's against what he teaches."

"Well, I'm not trying to get with him. I'm engaged."

"Now, don't get mad, but I don't think that's a wedding I will ever see. Darren is shady."

"You are my girl and you have never liked him, so I will excuse you on that."

"Well, you must admit I didn't like him when you first met him and guess what? What I felt was true."

"Whatever. I'm involved now."

"I love you, but I have to say this. Don't let that be your excuse. Remember, karma? When it comes back, it hurts twice as bad."

"I'll talk to you tomorrow. Love you and good-bye."

I knew Diana loved me and wanted me to do what was right; but I was doing what was right for me. Things would work themselves out. She was talking about karma and how it comes back. I didn't start this, but I was going to end it. Darren was the one. I let him go and he came back. That simply meant we were meant to be.

****

I was asleep when Darren came over. I'm not sure what time he finally came into the bedroom. But we had a couple of days left to be together and then his wife was supposed to be back. I couldn't help wondering if he was doing something with someone else. I mean, he hadn't been with me all evening, yet he didn't even wake me up. Was that what Diana meant about karma, or was that what Mother meant when she said I would always be suspicious of him because of what he did to his wife?

Chapter 18

When I woke up I was still a little upset that Darren had returned to my place so late. I could not imagine what he could've been doing that kept him in the office that long.

"Darren, we need to talk. I don't understand why you had to work into the wee hours of the morning, grading papers."

"I told you that it was the end of the semester and I had to submit the grades. Some of the students are graduating and needed their grades to assure that they would walk. Come here, girl." He grabbed me around my waist. "What do you think I was doing? I'm not doing anything that you would be angry about."

"You don't know the half of it."

"What do you mean by that?"

"Nothing, but I don't think I can handle this."

"Handle what? Me working? Now, I got enough of that crap at home from my wife, I am not about to go through it here."

I pulled myself from under his arms. "What do you mean?"

"Just what I said. I will not stand accused of doing something I'm not doing."

I grabbed my robe and attempted to walk out, but Darren grabbed me and started kissing me. "Please stop. I don't feel like this."

"Do you feel like this?" Darren traced his fingers over my breasts. I pushed them away. That made him angry. I tried to walk out of the room, but he snatched me back to him so hard my body hit his chest. He proceeded to pull my robe off and I struggled, trying to keep it on. "Stop! Please don't, Darren, please."

He kissed my tears away as he forced himself in. When it was over he kissed me as if I had invited him to invade my body with his liquids. I jumped and ran into the bathroom. Knocking on the door, he asked, "Are you okay, Denise? I didn't mean to hurt you."

I didn't answer because I was running my bath water. He stood at the door, pleading his love. "I love you so much, Denise. I'll never do that to you again."

He no longer was the man I fell in love with. He already took my heart and now he was taking my respect.

After I finished my bath, I dressed and he kissed me. When he walked into the shower, I left before he finished putting on his clothing. As I drove I saw that same white car, but no one was in it. It was parked three blocks from my house. But I kept driving. "Maybe I am seeing things," I say out loud.

I arrived at Jamestown mall. It was nearly eleven in the morning. I decided to find something to wear to my dinner with the pastor. I wasn't sure why I had decided to go. But I planned to go and enjoy myself. I shopped like I had no worries. I bought two black Jones of New York suits and a pair of Calvin Klein Nadine evening slides to go with my suit. Next, I searched for a black T-strap shirt. I found one with silver rhinestones on it. I stopped at a small café and ordered a small slice of chicken pizza and a cappuccino. Now I was ready for my dinner with the pastor.

I pulled into the driveway and opened the garage. Darren's car was gone. I ran into the house and took a quick shower, dressed and left for my date. I arrived at Pastor Davis' home at 4:55. I noticed that there were two other cars there. One had a Tennessee license plate, the other was from Missouri.

I rang the doorbell and Pastor Davis answered, "Hi, come right in."

"Hi, Pastor. How are you?"

"I'm fine and you?"

"Great!"

"Let's walk into the great room; I would like you to meet my family." We walked through a long hallway and then through the living room. We were both silent. As we entered the great room, two women stood up and walked toward me. One was either in her sixties or near it with beautiful salt-and-pepper hair. The other lady was much younger, maybe in her thirties.

"Sister Reese. Or may I call you Denise?" The pastor smiled and looked from me to the women.

"Denise is fine."

"Well, Denise it is. I would like you to meet my mother, Delores Davis, and my sister, Pamela Gary."

"Hello, nice meeting you, Ms. Davis," I said with a huge smile, extending my hand to her to shake. She nixed shaking my hand and grabbed me for a hug. "It's nice to meet you, too. You are such a pretty young lady."

"Thank you," I said embarrassed.

"This is my sister, Pamela. She has always played the role of my protector."

Pamela laughed. "That's right," she said. This is my baby brother and he may be a pastor and all, but I still have to watch his back." She walked toward me and we hugged. "Come on, sweetheart, have a seat next to me."

I walked over to the black Italian leather couch and sat next to her and Ms. Davis. I was a little nervous because I wasn't sure why I was there. Sure, I was attracted to Pastor Davis, who wouldn't be? He was handsome and the pastor of the church; I had found out that he had a successful computer firm and that he had a Bachelor's and Master's degree in computer science. Still, I wasn't sure why he had invited me to dinner, but I almost felt sure that what Sister Clay had been saying all along was true. Problem was, did I feel the same way since my heart was with Darren?

"What do you do for a living, baby?"

I turned to speak directly to Ms. Davis. "I am a senior manager with a social services agency. I help families and children locate resources to assure that they can remain intact."

"That's wonderful. Do you like working with children?"

"Yes ma'am. I love working with children and teens. I believe that with the right mentoring they can achieve so much."

"It was a person like you who inspired James. He used to go to the Boys Club and play basketball and other sports until this young lady...what was her name?" Ms. Davis snapped her fingers as if that very act would set off a fire and flame her memory. "James, baby, what was that lady's name who helped you?"

"Her name was Ms. Sharon."

"Yeah, she inspired him to learn how computers function and how to break them down. He graduated from Oakwood Seventh Day Adventist College and started his business while going into the ministry. He was called so young, I was afraid he would be like many young men who don't answer, but I always knew he would preach."

I smiled and looked at the pastor. He beamed and looked at me as if he had found his soul mate. While his mom was speaking, I wondered what his new impression of me was, now that Sister Clay had told him that I was seeing a married man.

Pamela jumped into the conversation. "What do you do in your spare time?"

"I read a lot. Mostly, inspirational and self-help books."

"Me too. My favorites are Romance though."

"Pamela, let's go get dinner ready and let them get to know each other better," Pastor's mother said as she stood, smoothed out her dress and pulled her daughter off the chair she was sitting in.

Pamela and Ms. Davis walked out of the room. For a few minutes, we were silent. I understood why. His mother had played the pastor's hand for him and he didn't want that to happen. He cleared his throat, not sure what to say next. I decided to call a spade a spade.

"Pastor, what are your intentions with me?"

He laughed. "You are straight to the point. Could you just, for today, call me James?"

"Yes, James." I smiled, showing all my thirty-two pearly whites. This made him more comfortable.

"Well, as you know I am single and as the pastor that can be difficult. When I first met you I honestly felt like there could be something there and I wanted to see if we could get to know each other."

"James, that day on the parking lot when you had to break up that argument, I'm sure you heard what Sister Clay said about me."

"Yes. I heard it. But I don't judge."

"But it is true." I looked at him. Our eyes met and I saw the pain. I felt it myself. It was difficult, but I had always been told that the truth would set me free. He was attracted to me, and I to him, but I was not available. I was in love with one man and attracted to another, but not enough to ruin what I already had.

There was a minute where time stopped. It was an awkward moment. I wasn't sure what to do or say. After what seemed like a suspension of time in space, he looked up from holding his head down. Our eyes met again.

"Do you plan to stay involved in that relationship?"

"He asked me to marry him after the divorce and I said I would."

"Well, that said, let's go have dinner."

What? Is that it? So you don't care about me. No fight?! No disappointment?!

"James, is that it? No questions?"

"Sister, you have made it clear that there is only one person in your heart and I have to let that be. I don't know what God has planned for my life or yours, but I have to trust Him and let His will work."

"You are not disappointed in me?"

"No, Denise. I'm not in a position to judge anyone and I won't try. Just know that I'm here for you if you need me."

With that he pulled me into his arms and hugged me. It felt comfortable there and I didn't want to let go, but I did. We walked into the kitchen to eat.

As we sat down, his mother said she would say grace. "I know this is your home, but I would love to have the honor."

It's been said that a mother knows her child. She knew her child's pain and her child's heart. I felt that Ms. Davis knew her son was disappointed, so she didn't want him to try to reach for prayer in our presence. I figured she wanted to comfort her child through prayer.

"Everyone, please bow your head." We all did as requested. "Father, please bless everyone at this table. I ask that You watch over these young folks and guide them in their everyday dealings. Work with them and help them to obtain those things that they desire if they are in Your will. If what they desire is not in Your will, help them to understand and to accept it. Thank You for this food that we are about to eat for the nourishment of our bodies. Give us all peace and good health. All these things we ask in Your name. Amen."

We all said, "Amen." I looked at Pastor James and he smiled. That made me feel much better. As the platters of food were being passed around, Ms. Davis asked if I had ever tasted vegetarian turkey. "Yes. I love it."

"Do you eat any other vegetarian food?" she asked as she took a forkful of dressing.

"Mostly, I eat it when there is a church function. My mother never learned to prepare it very well. Some of my favorites vegetarian foods are the Buffalo wings, turkey of course, and the Salisbury steak. A family friend makes excellent tuna salad, basically I eat vegetables and chicken."

"I'll have to prepare some other things for you to try. I think you would really like some of the other dishes."

"Mom, this vegetarian turkey and dressing tastes great," Pastor said, wiping the corners of his mouth with the napkin.

"Thank you, son."

"Pamela, do you live in Tennessee?" I wanted to know who was driving the car with the Tennessee license plates.

"Actually, Mom lives there and I live in Kansas City, Missouri. We both came to visit James and to spend some time with him. It's not often we get to see him since he moved here to pastor True Church. So every three months we come to visit."

"That's great. So, Ms. Davis, you drove here by yourself?"

"Nah, baby. Two of my church friends came with me, but they are spending time with their families. I could drive it by myself, but my son here won't allow it."

"It's just too far that's all, but Mom, you know I don't doubt that you could do it by yourself."

"Pass me the string beans," Pamela requested.

I passed the platter. "I love string beans and these are absolutely great."

"Well, that's good because my brother cooked them."

"In that case, I'll take another serving." We laughed as Pamela handed the platter back to me and I took a large scoop out and put it on my plate.

We talked about politics, education and the state of the country. We agreed on most of the topics. Ms. Davis served dessert. I took a small serving of the peach cobbler.

"Would you like some ice cream with that?" James asked.

"No thank you. This is fine."

After James and I helped clear the dishes away, I proceeded to help his mother and sister wipe the table off, but they sent me out of the kitchen. James took my hand and walked me through the kitchen toward the back of the house. "Let's walk out back. I need to walk this food down."

Once in the backyard, I pulled my hand out of his. "Thank you so much for inviting me to dinner. I have enjoyed myself. Your mother and sister are nice people."

"Thank you."

Silence invaded our space. I looked out toward the pool area. A second of time passed before another word was spoken.

"Did I tell you that you look beautiful?"

"I don't know. I can't remember. I get kinda nervous

A Sinner's Cry

around you."

"Really? Why?"

"I guess because you are a preacher."

"That should bring you some comfort."

"I just don't want to say something out of order."

He laughed. "What could you possibly say?"

I laughed. "Well, anything! I've been out of church for so long. Everything feels so new to me. It's like I am a baby again, trying to find my way. Things scare me."

"You don't have to be frightened. I'll help you, but nothing about loving God is frightening."

"I know. But—"

He put his finger to my lips. Shhhhhhh! You don't have to explain. I have been where you are and so have most people. We are all imperfect."

He kissed the top of my forehead. We stood there for a minute. No words were spoken as I held his hand firmly inside mine. I was confused. With him I felt mixed up like sugar mingling with salt, trying to find its way to separate. Tears came. He kissed them away. I looked up at him and he gently pressed his lips to mine. We kissed tenderly. But I pulled away quickly.

175

"I'm so sorry, but I have to go. I hope you find someone more suitable for you."

I ambled away as he reached out to pull me back, but I rushed into the house before another word could be spoken. As I wiped the remaining tears I entered the living room and thanked his mother and sister for such a wonderful meal.

"You're welcome. We really enjoyed your company."

"I enjoyed meeting you and Pamela. The meal was great and the hospitality even better."

"It was nice meeting you too, Denise." Pamela reached out to hug me and I hugged her back. I walked over to hug Ms. Davis and she held me tight. "Everything will be all right," she whispered into my ear.

"Thank you." I grabbed my purse. "Goodbye and thank you, James, for a wonderful evening."

"You're welcome. I'll walk you to the car." I slowed down and waited for him to walk toward me.

"Thank you, but that's not necessary."

"Don't be silly. I'll walk you." Taking my hand, James led me to the front door.

We strolled in silence. The silence was becoming too familiar. It was like a warm blanket that kept out the cold and the bad weather. Only it kept us from saying the wrong things. Things we were not sure the other was ready to hear.

"Thank you." I reached for the car handle. He reached, too. He towered over me, starring down into my eyes as if he was going to kiss me. I didn't want him to. I was so confused. Why was this preacher making me feel this way? Why was this happening when I had a man? I could smell his cologne. He smelled great and he was wearing this black suit like a male model, strutting on stage.

Suddenly, I reached up and kissed his lips. I couldn't resist it. My knees buckled. I pulled away, jumped into my car and backed quickly out of the driveway. "Lord, please help me. Why is that man so attractive to me? I am engaged. I am going to marry Darren." I looked through the rearview and he was still in the same spot, watching.

When I returned to my house Darren was there. He had just showered. He undressed me quickly and we made love like heathens. Only it was not his lips I kissed. I thought I was kissing him. I thought I was making love to him. I was screaming and moaning. When we finished making love, Darren rolled over. "Who is James?"

Chapter 19

The week went by quick. I spent the entire work week training staff on the No Child Left Behind law. This law was signed by former President George Bush in January 2002. The law, a landmark in education reform, was designed to improve student achievement and change the culture of America's schools. My department's task was to empower parents to help them become more involved in their children's educational experiences. We spent a lot of time training parents and teachers on ways to interact with each other and to become partners. Hours were devoted to developing and creating strategies and tools for parents and teachers, thus it had been a tedious and tiring week.

I planned to spend time at home, relaxing and reading for my own personal enjoyment. I would also attend church. Mother called earlier this morning and reminded me to bring the resource information for Sarah.

I arrived home and found at least twenty calls on my answering machine. The only messages left were heavy breathing. On the last call the message was brief. "Leave my man alone or I am going to hurt you." That was kinda scary to me. *I have to be more careful.* I ordered Chinese food. I was not doing anything tonight, but reading the Bible and trying to learn more about Jesus. I needed a refresher course. I was baptized at a young age and attended church regularly. If someone asked me about Jesus or the Bible I wouldn't be able to state answers. My mother always told her children that when it was necessary all of us would remember what we needed to, especially during times of trouble. That changed when the phone rang and it was Darren. He was coming over later to talk.

I ran my bubble bath and sat in the tub, reading and thinking. The phone jarred me from my thoughts. "Hello?"

"Happy Sabbath evening, Sister Reese."

"Same to you, Pastor."

"Our teen leader had to leave town for a family emergency, would it be possible for you to work with the teens tomorrow for the after-Sabbath rap session?"

There was silence as I contemplated what to say. It wasn't that I didn't want to work with the teens, it was the commitment and the uneasiness I felt about being back in church with my current lifestyle.

I broke the silence. "Pastor, I'm not sure that the teens should get used to me facilitating the group, especially with the rumors going around about me."

"I haven't heard any rumors, so I am not sure what you're speaking of."

A pause in the conversation was noticeable. I knew he was protecting me.

"Sister, can I count on you?"

"Yes," I finally said.

"Thank you and you have a pleasant Sabbath evening."

"You do the same." I was about to hang the phone up when

I heard his voice again.

"Sister, if you need me please don't hesitate to call me. Please."

"I can't imagine why I would need to call you."

"Just remember, I care about you."

"Thanks," I responded and hung up the phone before any more words could be exchanged.

Laying my head back on my tub pillow, I thought about the dinner we had the week before. I reached up to touch my lips and I could remember his soft lips on mine. The pastor and me, that was funny. A preacher's wife was something that I never aspired to be nor ever thought of. I was a good person who had made a bad decision, but even with that problem hanging over my head, I was still a good person, nevertheless.

I got out of the tub and dried off. I sprayed the tub with some 409, rinsed it out and turned the light out while going to the bedroom. After I put on my lounging pants and shirt I heard the doorbell ring. Rushing to answer it, I almost tripped over the rug in the living room. I peeped out and saw the delivery person with our food. Darren was standing there with him. When I opened the door, Darren asked the guy the cost, paid him and gave him a generous tip.

Walking into the door, he kissed me on the lips. "I can't stay. We need to talk."

I sat at the table and prepared our meal. After I prayed over our meal, I looked up and Darren had already started eating. Between bites, I asked, "What do you want to talk about?"

"Let's finish dinner first." Darren sat at the head of the kitchen table and I took a side chair.

Okay, now I knew that something was up. We ate in silence. After dinner we washed the dishes. Then he started to kiss me. I kissed him back. For some reason I knew that this would be the last time in a while we shared a kiss. We moved to the bedroom and made love like if we didn't, it would no longer exist. He was passionate. He kept saying my name over and over. We laid there and I asked again, "What do you want to talk about?"

"Jill wants to try again to save our marriage. I'm taking off for a while and we're going to the Bahamas to work on it. I hope you understand."

I laughed a nervous laugh. "What?" Now I was seriously pissed. He knew before he lay with me that he was going to try to work his marriage out. I guessed he wanted one for the road. "Please get out."

He got up, went into the bathroom and showered. When he returned I pretended to be asleep. He dressed and kissed me on the cheek. "I love you and I promise I'll be back to marry you. You have my word on that."

After he left I felt so used. I cried myself to sleep.

The pastor spoke on witnessing for Jesus. His message was simple. Jesus' life was an example of love and we should share His life and His love for all people to others. The pastor preached his heart out. Yet I could still feel his desire for a companion even in his message.

As we walked out I noticed how other women pushed to get to him. We made eye contact before I exited the receiving line and went out the other door. I decided I couldn't stomach those women hitting on him today. He had to have the patience of Job to resist all that temptation.

As I walked through the hallways and into the fellowship hall I heard a commotion. I walked toward the back and heard Sister Clay and this other lady whom I didn't know, arguing with each other.

"Sister Clay, I am so tired of you in my business. Get out of my face." The lady walked up to Sister Clay and their faces were almost touching each other.

"If I don't, what are you going to do?" Sister Clay was egging the woman on.

"Please get out of my face," she screamed. She pushed her out of the way.

"What are you going to do if I don't?" Sister Clay repeated as she walked closer to the woman. Then she shoved her back.

Next thing I knew they were swinging at each other. Left and right, they were throwing punches at each other. Sister Clay was getting the best of the poor lady until she slipped and when she did that sister tore her up. The elders of the church appeared and pulled the two ladies apart.

"Ladies, this is not Christian-like. You should both be ashamed."

"She started it," the lady said." It's hard being a Christian with the likes of her in the church."

With that, Sister Clay broke loose from Elder Bryant and dove on the lady again. Thus, they battled like boxers on the streets, except they were at church in front of a lot of Christians, teens and other struggling people. To say the least, it was embarrassing.

After they pulled the ladies apart a second time, the pastor walked up and spoke to the ladies and they disappeared into his study. I shook my head. I, too, felt like beating Sister Clay's butt, so I understood how the sister felt who had fought her.

I saw the youth pastor gathering all the teens together and he asked me to come with him. I did.

We had a quick session on what had happened. I ended up doing a discussion on conflict management. Not surprising, the teens understood the conflict and how it was not Christ-like to use your fist to solve problems, especially on the church grounds. We prayed with the teens and assured them that this was not the way that God intended for us to act. They felt better as they stated how stupid the adults looked fighting on the church's premises.

I returned to the church four hours later. There were three cars on the parking lot. Elder Bryant's, the pastor's and mine. I walked into the church and spotted Elder Bryant. "Hi, Elder Bryant."

"Sister Reese, thanks so much for facilitating that teen session today. It was so important for them to understand that what they saw at church today was not what God would want and should not be taken lightly."

"Yes, I do understand that."

"Since we held them already for more than an hour today, the youth pastor and his wife are taking the teens skating tonight, so you won't have a group tonight. But since you are here, the pastor and I would like to speak to you. Do you have time?"

"Sure."

"Follow me."

I followed him to the pastor's study. As I followed, I wondered what they could possibly want with me. When we entered the study, the pastor looked up from reading his Bible. He looked good. "Hi, Sister Reese. Please have a seat."

I sat down across from Pastor and Elder Bryant sat in the twin leather chair next to me. I folded my hands and got comfortable; I was not sure what they wanted.

"Sister Reese, the youth pastor and I wanted to ask if you would serve as a co-coordinator of the youth department. We understand that you have considerable skills working in the community as a leader and the teens respond so well to you. They need guidance and someone to mentor them with skills such as yours." Elder Bryant looked to the pastor.

"That's right, Sister, it makes all the sense in the world for you to co-head this position. I have been informed; you not only can help them with scholarships, but with employment opportunities, counseling and mentoring. You can also place them in corporations for internships. We need you. Our teens need you."

"Pastor Davis and Elder Bryant, I think I need to be honest with the both of you. I am a struggling Christian. I have been out of the church for a while and right now I am trying to learn about God's Word myself. I am trying to renew my relationship with God, so I'm just not ready to take on a Leadership role."

He looked at me with wonder, like I had a mask on and he didn't know about me. "I think you are a talented and well-respected young woman. Whatever issues you are struggling with, God will help you. Your life outside the church is important to your spiritual life, but I firmly believe that while you are working for the Lord, He will forgive and cleanse you. He will work with you on any other issues you may have. Sometimes, Sister, the best way to get to know God is to work for Him."

I bowed my head down and the tears came. I was so confused. I didn't even know why I was crying. Pastor looked at Elder Bryant and he excused himself from the room.

"Sister Reese, is there something you need to talk about?"

Shaking my head, I said, "No."

We sat there with me crying and him sitting across from me. He stood up and paced the floor. He walked over and sat close to me. "Is this about your relationship?"

"I'm so confused about so much."

"Is it something I can help you with?"

"No, Pastor."

"Then let me pray for you."

The pastor prayed the most beautiful, honest prayer for me. He asked God to give me peace and to help me with any problems or decisions that I needed to make. He asked God to work with me and to give me the desires of my heart. When the pastor finished praying for me, I thanked him.

"Please, Pastor, I need more time to think about this."

He squeezed my hand and said, "Take all the time you need, Sister."

When we walked out of the pastor's study, Elder Bryant was sitting in the Fellowship Hall. He walked over to us. "Is everything all right?"

"Elder, everything is just fine. Sister Reese will get back to us about the youth leadership position."

Elder Bryant smiled, showing beautiful white teeth. "That's fine."

"I'll walk Sister Reese to her car."

As we walked, the pastor asked if I would have dinner with him next Sunday. "I would like to cook you some more of my great-tasting string beans."

I started laughing. "Okay, since you said that, I would like to come to taste your great string beans."

"How about five o'clock next Sunday?"

"That's fine."

"Would you like me to pick you up?"

"No. I don't mind driving to you."

"Thank you. I'll see you later."

I got into the car and drove off. I was not sure if I was leading the pastor on, but I sure did want some of his string beans.

Chapter 20

I called Cynthia to discuss a course of action for her mother. Cynthia was going to help her mother get into a rehab center. Her goal was to move her to California, the following year. Sarah was adamant that she wanted to stay with her friends and church members. While I was on the phone, giving information to Cynthia, she dropped the phone.

"Mother, what are you doing with that? Please put it out."

In the background I heard shuffling. Then water running. Cynthia returned to the phone. "Mother was playing with fire. She's been drinking again. I don't know where she is getting this liquor from. I thought I had removed it all out of the house. She must have a secret stash."

"I'm so sorry that your mother is going through this. I didn't realize that it was so serious until I saw her at the restaurant."

"What restaurant?"

"About a month ago I went to Cracker Barrel and she was there. She had been drinking, so I took her car keys and drove her home. I returned later to get the car. That was the incident that made me call you."

"God is so good. He meant for you to see her; otherwise, we would have not known how serious her drinking was."

"God is good. All the time! Cynthia, whatever I can do to help, please, let me know."

"I will."

"Okay, let me give you the resources to contact. First, contact Call for Help. They will be able to assist you with any other information relevant to senior citizens." I gave Cynthia the phone number. I also gave her three numbers for rehab centers and the number to Senior Services to guide her to any other available services to help her mother.

"Thank you so much. This information will definitely help. I will contact you later to give you an update."

"Thanks. I appreciate that."

****

Monday morning started off rocky. I had a feeling that my day was going to be messed up. I wasn't sure how, but I knew something was brewing. At work I had to settle two serious arguments between staff members, which should have never happened in the office. Handling the altercations were time-consuming. It was so unnecessary since we were all professionals; nevertheless, it had to be done.

After clearing the air, mediating and getting everyone back on the same accord, we went back to helping parents and working with the students who had contacted us for help. Things settled down pretty quick and a lot of work was completed.

When I arrived home I noticed that my mailbox had been opened. I walked out of the garage to see why. Peering into the mailbox I saw a red piece of paper. I picked it up and the note read:

This is the last straw. If I catch you with my man again I'm going to kill you.

I did a full circle pivot to make sure no one was walking up on me. I then went into the house and contacted the police department. They came out and took a report. As usual, they wanted to know if I had any enemies and had I been involved in any conflicts. Again, I told them no. I reminded them of the broken window, the car following me and the harassing calls. They just told me to be careful, keep my security system on and to always couple myself with others until they, or I, could find the person harassing me.

Later that evening Darren came by. I had not seen him since he took the trip to the Bahamas to work on his marriage. Though I missed him, I could not stomach his presence. He was drunk. I wanted him out. He was not himself.

"Darren, please, let me call you a cab."

"I don't need you to call me a cab. I just need you."

"You are drunk. I don't even know how you made it to my house in one piece."

"Why haven't you responded to my calls?"

"Why should I? Didn't you say that you were trying to work on your marriage?"

"That didn't mean that I wanted you out of my life?"

"Then you are a fool. Why would I continue to see you when you want to save your marriage? As a matter of fact, I *am* calling a cab and I want you out."

With that, Darren slapped me so hard I fell backward in the hall chair. Then he hit me in my face several more times. While he was doing this, he tore off my clothing. He tried to rape me, but he was too drunk. I pushed him off me and picked up a lamp. He backed up and asked me to call the cab. "You are so stupid. I'm just too tired to beat your ass." He walked out the door. I slammed it and called him a cab.

After Darren left, I went to the bathroom to take a shower. I wanted to wipe off Darren's dirty hands. For now, I hated him. As I was drying off I noticed my reflection in the mirror. I had a black eye and my face was scratched. As tears fell they stung the scratches on my face. While I was drying off my face, I heard the screeching of tires. Grabbing a robe and putting it on, I rushed out of the bathroom to peep out of the front window. There was a huge bright red and yellow ball of fire all over a car. Darren's car was on fire. I called the fire department and they said that a fire truck was on the way. A neighbor phoned in the fire, too. I was so shaken. When the policemen arrived and took the report, Officer Percy said, "We are going to have to upgrade your case from harassment, to property damage" As he continued to talk, his words became slurred. I was losing it.

"Do you understand?" Officer McNeil asked.

"Yes." I was now concerned for my safety. As I sat there sobbing, Pastor Davis walked up to the door. When I saw him I dashed to him and fell into his arms. He was carrying a dozen of roses, which he dropped on the floor to hold me.

"Are you okay? What happened?" He wanted to know as he pulled me close to him.

"Yes," I whispered. "Everything happened."

He walked me to the couch and helped me to sit. Then he went to talk to the officer. After they talked, the officer walked over and gave me the report number and left. A tow truck came to remove the car. I was so shook up that I didn't remember agreeing to go to the pastor's house. After I packed a few things and contacted my office to let them know that I would be taking the rest of the week off, we locked down the house. As we walked out to the car, my cell phone rang.

"I'm on my way to pick up my car."

"Don't come, it has been towed," I said.

"Towed?! Why?"

"You might want to ask your wife that. She set it on fire."

"Are you crazy? Come on! I'm coming for my car." His voice was rising and it sounded throaty.

"It was set on fire!"

"I don't believe you; you need to stop playing games."

"Call the police department and they will verify this. Your wife is angry and you need to get control of this situation before someone gets hurt."

"Jill is not stupid or crazy. She would not do anything like that."

"A scorned woman will; you have pissed her off. Listen, you have hurt her and me badly. But the difference is she is your wife, so she is not only pissed, she is hurt and disappointed and that is a lethal mix."

"Jill would not stoop that low. I know my wife."

"Well, Darren, if she didn't do it, then you have a problem."

He was angry and confused. Still not wanting to believe that someone set his car on fire, he continued to deny it until I gave him the police department phone number and the report number. He was speechless. I disconnected the call.

Pastor Davis waited patiently until I completed my conversation. "Since your car is already in the garage, just leave it and I will drive."

"All right."

Pastor Davis led me to his car, opened the door and helped me get in. I was so shocked I just sat staring at nothing.

We drove forty-five miles in silence. When he pressed his keypad and drove into his garage, we sat there for a minute. He asked, "Are you okay, Denise?"

"Yes."

"You can stay here as long as you need to. I have plenty of room"

He closed the garage and we both got out of the car. We sauntered into the house and he led me to the guest room. It was beautiful. There was a gorgeous queen-sized sleigh bed draped in the most beautiful rose-colored bedspread. The curtains matched the bedspread and there was a beautiful huge executive-style cherry wood desk with a laptop computer ready to be used. There was also a matching Jack and Jill bathroom connected. I opened the other door leading to the next bedroom and it was decorated in Asian-inspired furniture, equally as beautiful. I shut the door and lay across the bed. I was in a bad situation, very confused, hurt and scared. Not only did I need prayer, I needed all the angels in Heaven and God because I was a mental mess.

I lay in bed for several hours and then I heard a soft knock on the door. "Denise, dinner is ready."

I got up and walked to the door and opened it. "I'll be down in a minute."

It was seven thirty. I washed up and went to the dinner table. "Hi," I said, as I sat in a cherry wood chair with a thick white padded seat and leaned on the table.

"Did you rest well?"

"Not really, but I do feel a little better. Thank you."

"You need an ice pack on your eye. I will fix you one after we eat." He placed a plate in front of me and then one in front of the chair he was sitting in. He had decorated the table with silverware and glasses. A large pitcher of lemonade sat near the center.

He offered prayer and asked God to bless both of us. Then he made some chatter about church activities and the upcoming conference that we were hosting in the fall. After dinner we went into the great room. He turned on the television and left me searching for something to watch. When he returned with the ice pack I was deep into *Law & Order*.

"Let me see if this will help. Does it hurt?" He pressed the royal-blue frozen rubber pad on my eye.

I jumped. "A little."

He got up, went back to the kitchen and returned with aspirin. I took two and he sat there holding the pack up against my eye until I relieved him. "The policemen wanted to know how you got the black eye. They said when you calm down they will need to talk to you to find out if this was all related in some way. How did this happen?"

"Darren hit me."

"Is that your fiancé?"

"Yes, he was."

Silence.

"Do you want to talk?" He put his hand under my chin and lifted it up to see my face.

"Pastor, maybe later, not right now." I shifted and turned to face the television.

I wanted to lie down because my eye was throbbing. "I'm going to turn in, if you don't mind."

"All right. Good night, Denise."

At 12:30 A.M. I woke up alone, scared and unfamiliar with my surroundings. I pulled the covers over my head to try to warm my body. Then I started sweating and shaking. I was having a bad panic attack. I jumped up, figured out where I was and then ran into James' room. He sat up. "Denise, what's wrong?"

"I don't know. I had a panic attack or a nightmare. Can I please stay in here with you?"

Through the darkness I saw the concern, the uneasiness.

"I don't think that is a good idea." He looked confused. I could tell he was trying to figure out how to handle the situation. But he ran out of time because I started crying. He looked sadly at me and then pulled the covers back for me to join him. He had on long pajamas, but even in the dark I saw his six-pack stomach. I spooned into him. He backed his body away from me. He whispered, "Everything is going to be okay."

I tried to fall asleep. I tossed and turned because I wanted more. I wanted him to make love to me. I wanted him to ease my fears and pain. I wanted to forget the man who had beat me. I wanted to forget the person who was haunting and harassing me. I turned to face him. He was staring up at the ceiling. He looked down at me.

I looked up into his eyes. He stared back. I reached up and kissed him. He kissed me back. First, we were passionate and then we kissed hungrily. I was ashamed about what happened next and I vowed never to disclose it. It was painful and embarrassing.

The next morning when I awoke he was gone. Deep down I knew he regretted bringing me to his home and not taking me to a hotel. I also knew the move that I made on him was wrong. That was probably why he left his room to get away from me. After I fell asleep, he left and slept in the guest room. I passed the door and saw the bed had been made up and his clothes where laid across it. I walked into the kitchen and there was a note that read he would be back later that night. It said to call him on his cell if I needed anything. He had fixed my breakfast.

After eating I called my mother and she arrived to pick me up. I left a message thanking him for his hospitality. I had to leave his home. I was so ashamed of my actions.

****

I returned to work one week later after recuperating and staying the rest of the previous week at my mother's house. I decided to move. No need of returning to a house that provided me with nothing but so much pain lately. I also decided that I was not going back to church. I was so ashamed about my bedroom antics that I could not face Pastor Davis.

I spent the next month searching for a new house. I saw Darren and he pleaded for me to forgive him. I just couldn't, even though I still loved him. I may have been a fornicator, a home-wrecker and some even called me a whore, but I refused to become a victim of domestic violence. In addition, I had begun to care a lot for Pastor Davis. I was so confused, I decided to swear off men until I could get my self-control back.

I was working in my office when I received the strangest call from the receptionist. She informed me that I had a visitor by the name of Trisha Coates. I wondered if she was the same Trisha from The True Church.

I walked to the front to meet her, and it was. "Hi, Trisha."

"Hi, Denise."

I led her to my office. "Have a seat." I pointed to the chair in front of my desk. "What can I do for you?"

"I came by to ask you a question and I want you to be honest with me. I know that this is not the right place to come to, but I wasn't sure you would be at church Saturday and plus I couldn't wait."

"What do you want to know?"

"Sister Clay said that she saw you leave the pastor's house

last Tuesday. She said it was early in the morning."

"Sister Clay talks too much. Apparently getting her butt beat didn't quiet her down."

Trisha laughed. "I guess not."

"Why is my life your concern?"

"Because I love him."

"You love who?"

"Pastor Davis."

"Pastor Davis?" I repeated with my eyebrows pointed up in disbelief.

"Yes. Pastor Davis. I've loved him ever since I came to the church. He was the one who invited me to attend. I met him at the college when I was enrolling to work on my GED. He was so nice to me. Nobody has ever treated me like I was important. At first when I started coming to church he did all my Bible study classes, then he asked the Women's Ministry team to take over. I was so hurt, but I still love him."

"Does he know how you feel? I mean, have you told him?"

"Yeah, I tried to, but when I was telling him, he stopped me and told me that he was the pastor and he was not interested. He said that he was flattered and after that he pretty much stayed away from me."

"He doesn't mistreat you, does he?"

"No. He's not like that. He's nice. I just want more. He's young, single and free, at least I hope so."

I laughed. "Well, I am not dating him."

"Did you sleep with him?" Trisha was drumming her fingers on the arm of the chair she was sitting in.

"Sorry. That's none of your business." I leaned back and put the end of my ink pen in my mouth.

Trisha was on a mission. She was not about to give in. "Are you interested in him?"

"That's none of your business either." I leaned forward and said, "I have work to do."

I stood up to let her know the conversation was over." You know what? You should mingle with the women's group and spend more time with them. Sister Clay gossips too much and you are trying to learn about God and become saved. You don't need to be straddling the fence and dealing with this crazy stuff. Maybe if you change your attitude and change the way you dress—"

Interrupting me and getting an attitude, while looking at me as if she could chop me in half, she asked, "What's wrong with my clothes?" She stood up, turned and modeled her clothing. Then she sat back down.

"Nothing if you are in the street, looking to party. I just

think if you change the inside, you should also change the outside. Then I think you will attract the man you want."

"Would you help me?"

"Yes, but you have to start attending the young adult group on Sabbath evening."

Trisha surprised me. She was calm and smart. She knew when to back off and she decided to get help rather than stay in the same place, going nowhere. I was about to walk her out, promising to work with her. She said that she and her friends would attend the teen rap meeting.

"I don't hate you," she blurted out.

"That's good. But I never thought you did."
She stood up to leave. "I was jealous because I thought you were taking my man away from me, but you are pretty cool, Sister Reese."

"I would be careful saying the pastor is your man unless he asks you to be his woman. It's not fair to jeopardize his respect and his ministry." When I uttered the words I thought about my own self. The night I went home with him, I should have respected his space. I'm sure he wanted to take me to a hotel, but sometimes when you care about a person you want them close to you, so you are assured they are protected. You don't think how things look to those looking from the outside. I know he was thinking with his heart and not his head. I should have been more thoughtful of his position. I, too, had jeopardized his ministry with my want-to-make-love antics.

"You are right. I'll stop until he asks me, then it's on."

"That's funny." I laughed. She laughed and I felt better.

Chapter 21

I woke up in my bed, sweating again. I dreamed that a young lady was making love to Darren. I couldn't see her face, but they were fully into the act. She turned and looked into my eyes, but her eyeballs were bright green. When she smiled, her teeth were as sharp as a tiger's. Her nails resembled long, white hard claws. As Darren pressed his body into hers, she pushed her claws into his back. The red blood flowed out like a stream of water flowing back into its riverbed. She laughed and mouthed the words, "You are next."

I jumped out of bed and switched the light on. Even though I was at Mother's house, the dreams hadn't stopped. I could not make light of the situation any longer. Darren was history. My dream was trying to tell me something.

It was five in the morning. I boiled hot water for my decaffeinated tea. After drinking the tea I got ready for work. As I was preparing to walk out of the door, the phone rang. It was Sister Clay.

"I need to talk to you."

"I have nothing to say to you." I held the phone securely. *Why does she irk me so?*

"You will talk to me or the board of the church. I saw you leave the pastor's house with clothing. You were getting into your mother's car. I think that was inappropriate for you and the pastor to act like you are stupid teens. He is the pastor and we look up to him and you are going to make him the laughing stock of the church."

"I don't have time for you. Tell the board whatever you need to. While you are at it, tell them how you have been harassing me and the pastor. I mean you are spying on him and calling and hanging up on me. What? You want the Pastor, too?"

"You are sick. You are a witch and I am going to get you thrown out of the church and if the pastor is sent packing, too, so be it. He shouldn't think with the wrong head."

I hung the phone up and laughed my way to the car. I drove to the gas station. While I was pumping my gas into the car, a young lady of about twenty walked over and asked me directions to the university. I gave them to her, but I didn't feel that she was paying attention to what I was saying. She kept watching me as if she was trying to see through me. Even though she tried to be nice, I felt like she was pretending. Her eyes seemed cold, with her steely black irises, yet she tried to act warm. She got back into her car, but she stayed until I pulled off. When I checked my rearview mirror she was following me instead of following the directions I had given her. When she saw that I was watching her, she turned the corner.

I didn't think she was the person who had followed me on a couple of occasions because she was driving an olive green Buick, but that was weird.

As I drove to the office and parked on the lot I saw Darren getting out of a new Mercedes. *Will he ever leave me alone?*

He took long-legged strides to get to me. "Hi, Denise."

"Hi, Darren." I got out the car and hit my keypad to set the

206

alarm.

"I stopped by to see how you are doing. I miss you," he said as he leaned in to kiss me.

Jumping back as if I was dodging a baseball, I responded, "Yeah, right."

"Seriously, I meant you no harm. You know how I feel. I didn't mean to hit you. I am so stressed out with the marriage, you and work problems. Please understand."

"Understand what?"

"That I have to take care of all these problems and then you and I can get married."

"Please! You don't still think I'm interested in marrying you, now do you?" I took off walking and he followed.

"You said you loved me. Why would I not think you wanted to marry me? You took my ring."

"Yeah and that was because you lied. No! I am not going to marry you. I wish you would go back home to your family."

"Please, Denise, let's talk about this."

"I am warning you. If you come back around me at my house or job, I am personally going to visit your wife."

"You are so stupid." He tried to block my path.

"Yes I am for messing around with your two-timing self." There was so much anger in him. I wondered what happened to him. He was not the same.

I remembered that Darren had beaten me. With that thought, I took off running to the building. When I looked back he was getting into his car with an extremely angry look on his face.

****

I spent the morning returning calls to business associates. As I prepared to write a grant, the receptionist interrupted my progress. "Good morning, Ms. Reese."

"Good morning, Ms. Jenkins. How can I help you?"

"Sorry to interrupt you, but you have a call on line one. Her name is Trisha Coates."

"Thank you." I clicked her off and pushed line one. Good morning, Trisha. How are you?"

"Hi, Denise. Please don't get mad. I'm calling you because Sister Clay is calling a board meeting about you and the pastor. I just thought you should know."

"Thank you so much, Trisha, but please, there is no need to worry."

"All right."

"I'll talk to you later."

"Are you going to be okay?"

"Don't see why I wouldn't be, but I'm okay. Talk to you later. Bye now. Oh, Trish, thank you."

"You're welcome. Bye."

I sat at my desk and laughed. This was funny to me. I just hoped the pastor would survive. I could deal with the jealousy of women. But the pastor might be out of his league. I wasn't going to be worried. Sister Clay had a reputation and that would be considered before all else anyway.

The rest of the day I worked on the grant and fielded phone calls. As I was preparing to leave, my cell phone rang. It was Darren. Initially, I was not going to pick it up, but decided to see what the man wanted.

"Denise, please meet me at your house."

"No, Darren. What part of, I am not interested in you, are you not getting?"

"Calm down. I just want to talk, okay?"

"Actually, there is not much to talk about."

"Please let me make it up to you. Jill did not burn the car. Somebody else did and I think I know who."

"Then call the police." I hung up on him.

Chapter 22

The rest of the week went by uneventful. Pastor Davis called the house as well as my cell phone more than five times, but I had no intention of calling him back. I knew that seemed disrespectful, but that was me. I was embarrassed about getting into his bed. In my right mind I would have never done such a thing, but I wasn't in my right mind; I was sinning. I was in a violent relationship that I was trying hard to get out of and I was being harassed by an angry, hurt and disappointed wife. So no, I was nowhere near having a right mind. I couldn't face the pastor when I had done the unthinkable. I mean, I got in his bed and spooned myself into him as if we were husband and wife, or lovers. I could not face the man that I had put in the position to sin, to lose his soul by fornicating with me. I refused to talk to him or put myself in another embarrassing situation.

On Friday my beautiful mother called me. She wanted me back in church and she wanted it tomorrow. Shaking my head, "Mom, how can you call me and try to make me go to church?"

"Because I am your mother and I said so."

I held the phone, trying to think of what to say next. That was a feat in itself. With everyone else I could shoot words off as fast as bullets leaving a gun's chamber, but with my mother I always experienced a loss for words. But what could you say when your mother was telling you what she wanted you to do? You listened and obeyed, even if you were a grown woman.

"You can't hide from him."

"Mother, I am not trying to."

"You spent the night at his house and I trust that the two of you refrained from acting on impulses, but that's y'all business and I have nothing to do with that."

"Mother, don't worry yourself."

"I'm not worried. I am concerned that Pastor Davis may have fallen for the wrong girl. Not that you are not good enough, but you are still seeing a married man."

"Not really. I broke that off."

"But it is not really over yet?"

"It is, Mother."

"I hope so. Now back to what I called you for. I want you at church tomorrow and I am inviting a few guests over for dinner."

"Okay. I guess."

"I'll see you tomorrow." Mother hung the phone up.

I hung up the phone that I was using and laid my head into my hands. I had been spending the last week at my own house, having to pack my things before putting them into storage. Diana was staying with me to help. I walked into my home office and asked Diana would she go to church with me the following day. She agreed.

****

Saturday morning was so beautiful, sunny and bright. The sun was giving off heat that seemed to beam in every spot I stood. I put on a crisp, white, cotton dress with T-straps and a short matching jacket. I also slid my feet into some sexy silver-and-white sandals with rhinestones across the ankle and across the front strap. Diana wore a soft yellow two-piece short sleeve suit. We looked fresh, cool and pretty. I also packed another outfit for later because I was scheduled to work with the teens after the sun set.

We arrived at the True Church; the first person I saw was Sister Clay. She stared at me like she wanted to burn a hole through my soul with her angry eyes. I politely walked past her. As Diana and I entered the front door of the church, Trisha walked up to me and hugged me. I hugged her back.

Holding her hands, I asked, "Are you coming to the group tonight?"

"Yes, I'll be there."

"Trisha, this is my friend, Diana."

Diana extended her hand to her and they shook hands. "Nice meeting you," Diana said.

"Nice meeting you, too," Trisha said. "Actually, I've seen you here before, but under worse circumstances."

"I know."

Just then the usher walked up and started talking to Diana. I stood and waited. I knew that they were welcoming her to the church and getting her information. Diana had attended church with me before. So this wasn't new to her.

Once we were seated in the church, the pulpit speakers walked in and we stood up. The pastor, two elders and two teens were speaking today. As we sat back down, one teenager walked up to the pulpit and told us to turn to Matthew 24:4. He read the verse to us as we followed. The pastor and I looked at each other and he smiled. I didn't smile back because I didn't want him to think that I was over what had happened.

Church was filled with the Holy Spirit. I felt revived. I felt happy and I could tell that everyone had been touched by the Holy Ghost. People were walking around, hugging each other, and wishing each other well. Smiles were pasted everywhere. I felt so good and Diana was being welcomed and treated with so much hospitality, I felt that she would pass out from the overabundance of love.

As we moved through the receiving line to greet the pastor and his pulpit members, people were walking up to the line still hugging and talking. As I neared the pastor, he was thanking Diana for coming back and he glanced at me. I was sure he didn't know how I would respond to him.

"Hi, Pastor," I said with fake confidence. Averting my eyes away from his, he asked me how I was doing.

I saw my best friend, Sister Clay, staring at me. "Nice seeing you, Sister Reese. Will you be here tonight with the teens?"

"Yes. I'll be here."

"Good. Good to see you, Sister Diana. Please feel free to visit again. You are no longer a guest."

"Thank you, Pastor." Diana shook his hand and gave him a great big toothy smile.

Diana and I left church after meeting and greeting most of the members. Sister Clay pretty much stayed away from me. She didn't seem to be a happy camper because I didn't see her mingling much. She stayed to herself mostly. I even felt sorry for her. I knew the members were staying away from her after that fight. Plus, I heard that she had sent a letter to the board about me. Mother had said that the board was not going to act on it.

We left the church and headed to my mother's house. Once there we washed our hands and helped to set the table. As I was making sure that the food was hot enough, the doorbell rang. Mother answered it.

I heard the voices, but didn't know who Mom had invited over. To be truthful I didn't care. Mom moved the people to the den area and Diana and I continued to prepare for the dinner. After we had set the table for six, I walked to the back to let everyone know that the food was ready. As I entered the den, my mouth flew open, my eyes bucked and I gasped. There sitting on the couch next to mother were Pastor Davis, Elder Bryant, Elder Grant and Deacon McKinley. Deacon Anthony McKinley was a young man, maybe in his early thirties; he was a doctor. He, too, was single, handsome and highly sought after as husband material by the single women of the church. He was a tall man, bi-racial, having a black mother and white father. His dental practice was in the Fairview Heights area, which was a hop, skip and a jump from East St. Louis.

I spoke to everyone, but I could tell from the looks on their faces that they knew I didn't expect the pastor to be there. This was because as soon as I walked through the door I nearly dropped the tray I had in my hands as I stopped in my tracks. I was bringing the tray to collect the glasses Mom passed out when everyone arrived. "The dinner is ready."

"That's good news, Sister," said Elder Bryant.

On their way to the dining room the visitors all stopped in the restroom and washed their hands. My mother looked at me and chuckled. She had this all planned. I guess since I wasn't talking to the pastor when he called me, mother had this dinner to put me in the position to talk to him.

Mother led the way toward the dining room. I stepped to the side and let the others pass me. The pastor was the last in the room. The others proceeded through the hallway. As I waited on him to pass me, he stopped.

"Denise, when are you going to stop avoiding me?" He reached for my hand and held it in the palm of his.

"I'm not avoiding you."

He reached out and pulled me by the elbow to the side of the room away from the doorway. "I have been calling and calling and you haven't responded."

I stood there. I didn't know what to say. He was right. I was avoiding him. We stared at each other. No words were spoken, but feelings were intense. Deep. I could feel the emotions in the room. His chest was rising up and down. His eyes were not blinking. I was uneasy. I held the tray so tight I looked like a statue.

"We need to talk."

"I know." I looked into his eyes. They were full of concern. He was still holding my elbow.

"You're shaking. I would never hurt you intentionally."

He was right on target. Being this close made me nervous. The glass started rattling on the tray. I pulled my hand away from him. As I did he walked closer to me. There was no space between my face and his. This was uncomfortable, but nice.

"Tomorrow, I would like for you to go to the Arch with me and to lunch. I'll pick you up at twelve."

"Okay." No more words escaped me. I smiled. He did, too. Then we both walked into the dining room.

Mother prepared two different meals. She had turkey and dressing, baked macaroni and cheese, collard greens, peas, sweet cinnamon carrots, cakes and sweet potato pies. For the vegetarians, she had a meatless lasagna, string beans, collard greens without meat and a bean casserole. There was so much food. Everyone was excited and ate as much as their bellies could take. There was a lot of movement at the table. Silverware clattered. Platters were passed around. Napkins were picked up often. I looked across the room and saw that Diana and Deacon McKinley were having a one-on-one conversation, as if they were the only two in the room. It was refreshing to see that Diana had possibly found someone.

The pastor appeared happy and confident. He was chatty. Smiling. Mother had a look of utter satisfaction on her face. She laughed often and winked at me several times. Even I had relaxed. Mother's dinner worked, maybe too well. Had she planned to be a matchmaker for Diana, too? I didn't tell her that I was bringing her. But still Mother probably invited Deacon McKinley this morning.

Dinner was marvelous and the conversation was great. Everybody rose from the table, patting their bloated stomachs and adjusting their clothing. Almost everybody stretched in some form. Once it was over, Diana and I washed the dishes and cleaned the kitchen. After we put the food away, we went into the den and finished talking with the guests. After three hours, the guests left. Diana and I rested.

After a full day, Diana and I left to go work with the teenagers. Trisha was there. Both teens and young adults from ages thirteen to twenty-one were in attendance. It was a great group. Trisha fit in well. She seemed happier and relaxed.

When the group session ended, Diana and I returned to my house. I was looking forward to my date. Diana and Deacon McKinley had agreed to go out. She was looking forward to her date as well.

Chapter 23

"Diana, how does this look?" I had slipped on my blue jeans, sandals and a fitted light-blue shirt.

"You look great in that outfit. I don't know why you don't wear jeans more often. You have the best shape."

"Do you think my shirt is a little short? I have a little stomach out." I patted my flat stomach.

"That's fine. It's the style. Plus, you don't have it all out. I think he will appreciate you looking a little sexy, but not too much."

"Okay. It does look cute, but remember he is a preacher." She pulled my shirt down a little.

"He's a man, girl. They like the same things."

We laughed. I combed my hair and changed purses. I opted to take a small blue jean purse. I was beginning to fall for the pastor.

"Diana, I see that you and Deacon McKinley are talking on the phone a lot. He's called three times since the dinner. What gives with him? I mean you just met him yesterday."

"He knows what's good for him, that's all."

"Do you like him?"

"Who wouldn't? He is nice, intelligent, successful,

handsome and single."

"So are you all planning on a date this week?"

"Yes, this coming Saturday after sunset. Okay, explain this sunset thing to me again."

"Okay. In Exodus chapter twenty, verses eight through eleven, the Bible says to remember the Sabbath day and to keep it holy. It also says that God made the heaven and earth, sea and all that is in them and rested on the Sabbath Day. It further says that thou should not do any work, or have anyone to do anything for you, because the Lord blessed the Sabbath and hollowed it. So simply put, when the sun goes down on a Friday night to sundown Saturday, that is the Sabbath. Now the Bible says six days shall you do all thy work and rest on the seventh day. Now you think, what is the seventh day of the week? Well, the Bible makes references about it throughout. But even if you look in the dictionary for what is the first day of the week, it will say Sunday. I even looked in the encyclopedia and it too said Sunday. When I looked up what the seventh day is, the dictionary and encyclopedia both said Saturday, so without even getting verification from the Bible, those two support the Sabbath as Saturday."

"Well, that is so deep."

"I realize that it is a lot to understand. After all, most people, including myself, until we found out the truth, went to church on Sunday. Jesus and His disciples observed Saturday as the Sabbath because that was so important to God."

"I know that you have to go on your date, but if Saturday is the Sabbath and people go to church on Sunday, why are folks breaking God's law?"

"For one thing because that's what they know, so many have been taught that Sunday is the Sabbath. The change came by Roman Catholics and then later the Orthodox Greek churches. They changed the Saturday Sabbath to the Sunday Sabbath. But when you read the scriptures it says that God's Word is, and was and will always stay the same. So in my book no man can change God's laws or commandments."

"Wow. That is deep because the majority of Christians are practicing on a day that is not sanctioned by God." Diana twisted her thumbs as if she was in deep thought.

"Well, change is hard. Think about it, most folk have been attending church their entire lives on Sunday. I know so many folk who know the right day, but refuse to practice it. For me, I want to follow God's law, not man's.

"Would you give me the other Bible verses so that I can learn more?"

"I can do better than that; I can attend Bible classes with you. I have some things I need to change to remain in favor with God. You know I have been seeing a married man and that is so wrong. Plus, I haven't been keeping the Sabbath or nothing else holy, so I'll go with you."

"But you didn't know he was married."

"But when I found out, I stayed. It's the same with the

Sabbath, people say they don't know, but when they learn the truth they don't change. It's because of habits, comfort zones and doing what they know. But I want to live right and to do that I have to let Darren and all of his mess go."

Diana hugged me. "I don't want to be lost on a technicality. I want to follow God, not man. I think the pastor is here. I just saw his Mercedes pull up."

"Okay. We can start Bible classes at the end of the month. But in the meantime, feel free to ask Deacon McKinley. After all, you're getting to know him and I am sure that he will want you to understand him and what he believes in."

"I'll mention it to him, but for right now you leave," Diana said as she pushed me toward the front door.

"Okay," I said abruptly, stopping. "Thanks, Diana, for staying here with me and for dealing with all my craziness."

"You are my best friend, plus Darren and that wife of his are crazy. Darren has already called five times today. You are going to have to put an end to this foolishness."

"I know and I will soon."

"I'll see you this evening."

Chapter 24

Pastor rang the bell and I opened the door and greeted him. He smiled as if he had just won the lottery.

"Hi Pastor James." I said as I walked out the door and with him to the car.

"Please call me James," he reminded me.

"Okay, as long as you don't call me Sister."

He laughed. It does sound old on you, since you are so young."

"Yes, and you and your church folk need to come up with something that fits the under-forty crowd."

"Well, you know that is the title."

We continued to chat as he opened my door to let me into the car. "I've been living here almost six years and I have never been to the Arch. Let's go there or would you rather eat first?"

"No, let me show you around the Arch and the grounds there, and then we can eat at one of the cafes down on the riverfront. Do you know how to get there?"

"I'm sure I can find my way, Denise. But you let me know if I do something wrong? By the way, you look nice in jeans."

"Oh really?"

We both giggled like teenagers with a bad crush on each other. When we arrived at Laclede's Landing, which was an area in downtown St. Louis that hosted the Arch and some neat little historical restaurants and shops, we parked. As we walked up what seemed like a hundred steps I pointed out the riverboats and the Geyser. The Geyser was a water fountain located in East St. Louis near the riverbanks of the Mississippi River. The water that shot out squirted taller than the Arch.

We entered the Arch and I gave James a first-rate tour.

"James," I said, "the Arch is six-hundred-thirty feet tall. People come from all around the world to ride to the top. The top of the Arch is where you'll get a great view of the St. Louis region."

James was impressed and looked all around like a kid at a circus for the first time. "How do you get to the top?"

"That's the fun part. You take a tram ride from the south or north leg of the Arch. Come on, let's ride up."

Once we got into the tram, James grabbed my hand and held it tightly. It felt nice. "This is a little bumpy."

"Yeah, but not too bad." He smiled as we headed up higher.

Once at the top, we peered through the tiny windows. It was weird to see people at the bottom of the Arch. They looked like little ants. Then we traveled back down and I took him in to view the documentary on the making of the Arch. It was interesting. When that was over we walked around, touring the museum store. This was indeed an out-of-this-world experience. Then we walked around the landing.

"How did you become so knowledgeable about this place?"

"You really don't want to know; long story. I have studied the history of the Arch and the Laclede Landing for school papers. Plus, I bring groups here often from our programs for the company I work for."

We walked on the cobblestone streets and through the century-old brick buildings, browsing in the specialty gift shops. James purchased a stuffed bear for me, with the caption, *I like you.* Finally, we decided to eat at Jake's Steaks. I'd never been to that restaurant, but had heard that they served great pasta. As we sat there, horse-drawn carriages passed by.

"I want to do that someday." I looked at him with a huge smile.

"You want to today?"

"No. I think you have to schedule it. It costs about forty-five dollars for thirty minutes."

"Okay, I would like to try that with you." He scooted closer to me and kissed me. I almost melted like ice on a hot-burning sidewalk. We looked into each other's eyes and I wanted to say something, but nothing came out.

"You and I need to talk about some things, especially about that night."

Not about the night that I slipped into your bed and put you in a bad position. Not the night that I pushed myself on you, willing and ready to give myself to you. I ruined the mood by saying, "I don't want to discuss it."

"Eventually we'll have to. Things need to be said. Feelings need to be soothed."

I pushed my plate away and prepared to stand up and leave. Grabbing my arm, he said, "Don't leave."

He was looking and pleading with me with beautiful brown eyes that made my heart simmer and melt, releasing tender thoughts and passion. I sat down. Bending my head down, I whispered in a child-like voice, "I'm not ready."

"I can wait." He kissed my cheek and pulled my plate back in front of me. "I'm enjoying being with you. Would you go to the Cardinals baseball game with me Thursday? I have some great box seats."

"Really? I would love to."

"The game starts at seven. I can pick you up after you get home from work."

"That's fine."

We finished our meal and arrived back at my house at six. I had spent six hours with him and enjoyed his company. When we arrived, he hopped out of the car and opened my door like a gentleman. He walked me to the door, holding my hand. At the door I turned to thank him and met his lips. We stood their kissing for about five minutes. Well, it was more like two minutes, but the effect he had on me made me think it was longer. I went into the house and he left.

Chapter 25

Walking into the front door and locking it, I spun around in a circle, singing, "I Got a Love Jones." I heard someone knocking and ran to open the door, thinking it was Pastor James. I opened it without looking.

I screamed out of fear; I knew I was in trouble.

"Darren! What are you doing here?"

"I've been waiting in the car for you to come home and what do I see, you kissing another man," he said walking quickly toward me.

"Please, get out," I said as I backed up.

"You are a whore. I thought you were a nice woman. But this!" He swung his hands toward me.
"Darren, I don't want any trouble. Just leave, please." I turned to run, but he grabbed me.

"Not until you give me what I came for." Darren rushed toward me with exaggerated hand-and-arm movements. He was preparing to subdue me against my will. As he grabbed my arm and twisted it toward the back, the front door swung open and Diana screamed, "Anthony, help!"

Diana had spent the day with Anthony. I guess they got tired of talking on the phone and he came to take her out. Diana rushed toward us, and Darren told her to back off. "Let her go," she hissed as she pushed him hard.

"Get back, Diana, this is between me and Denise."

Anthony thrust the door open. He hurried toward Darren, frightening him and he released my arm.

"I have no quarrels with you, brother. This is between me and my lady." Darren stepped away from me.

"I'm not your lady, get out!"

"Man, she asked you to leave. I think you need to oblige."

Anthony's look changed from upstanding, professional to a thugged-out street fighter. This proved to me what they said about men who hit women; they would not fight a man.

"I just want my ring," Darren said as he began to move toward the door.

Diana stood by me and said, "Give him the ring, Denise."

"No. It's mine for the trouble."

"Denise Maria Reese, give him the ring now!"

I turned and headed to my purse, after retrieving it from my wallet I handed the ring to him. He looked at me, mouthed the word" bitch" and stepped out the door.

"Hey, man, don't come back around here." Anthony walked him out.

"Diana, you came in the nick of time. I don't know what that crazy man was planning on doing to me. But the ring was mine."

"Denise, nothing is more important than your life. That ring was not worth the trouble."

"I guess so."

Anthony came back in and informed us that Darren claimed that he was through with me.

"Good riddance," I said.

I thanked Anthony, and gave both him and Diana a hug before I went to my room to shower and change into some more comfortable lounging clothing. I had stopped calling him Deacon unless we were at church. When I returned to the living room area, Diana was on the phone, laughing and talking to her man. Anthony left while I was in the shower. So I assumed he was on his cell with her. I went into the den and turned on the television. It was almost time for one of my favorite shows, *Cold Case*.

I was thankful because I was a praying sister when I opened that door and saw Darren. I prayed that God would help me and He sent Diana and Anthony back to the house. Diana told me that she was worried about me because Darren kept calling even after I had left. She felt that he would show up. To me, I knew that God understood and was always prepared. He understood our problems and knew our needs. He knew that Darren was coming over, so He put Diana and Anthony there to protect me. God also knew that I wanted out and was fighting to live my life for Him.

Around eight that evening Pastor Davis called and I told him what had happened. He wanted to come to me, but I told him that I was safe and okay. He was concerned about me and prayed a beautiful prayer that God would watch over Diana and me. I was falling and I had nothing to hold onto to ease the landing.

****

My second date with the pastor was even better than the first. Going to the baseball game allowed me to see him in a different light. He was a fun person to be around. He was so animated about the Cardinals and spent a lot of time talking at them like he was their coach. I found him so sexy. He had on a pair of jeans and a black T-shirt that hugged him in the right places. Plus, it didn't hurt that the man had a body that looked like he took it out of a magazine and pasted it on. You couldn't tell that he was a preacher. The women at the game were admiring him hard. Pastor Davis had that look. His appearance spoke loudly of class, money and status. There were some people who mastered the look of success and there were those who thought they were and trust me, I could tell who the real deal were.

Pastor kissed me several times in plain view of others, so I knew he was feeling me and was not hiding me. He liked me and enjoyed my company, and I, for the first time felt comfortable enough to grab his hand and hold it. I think it shocked him because he looked at me and then broke out into a one-hundred-watt smile.

After the Cardinals won the game, we drove to the county, not too far from my home for a light dinner. We decided to go to Denny's since it was still open. We talked about everything and about nothing. We really learned a lot about each other. Afterward, he drove me home and we sat in the car like teenagers, necking for more than thirty minutes.

"You better go in. Muah!" He kissed me again.

"Why, Pastor, you can't stand the heat?"

"No, and you can't either." He kissed me again, and then jumped out of the car. He opened my door and walked me to the house. This time he was watching for movement, other cars and people sitting. I knew he was making sure Darren wasn't around watching. We kissed at the door. Then he said, "Go in, lock the door and don't open it without asking who it is."

"Okay." I kissed him again. I did not want him to leave. If I had my way, I would've dragged him to my bed, but I was being a good girl.

I found Diana, as usual, on the phone. I bent down and kissed her cheek. She covered the phone. "What's that for? You must be in love. I don't recall you ever kissing me."

"Good night, girl."

I walked into the bedroom, showered and slept. I dreamt of the pastor holding and kissing me. As he slid his hand down to remove my underwear, the phone rang. It was the woman.

"You whore, you hurt my man. It's on."

I hung the phone up. *This is stupid. Tomorrow I will change my phone number. I can't wait until I move.*

Chapter 26

Good news, I sold the house. Diana and I were moving small boxes into the car to put into storage. It took three months, but I knew it would sell fast because it was so spacious and had plenty of room for a growing family. It was late July. The pastor and I had been seeing each other weekly. Mostly we went to activities away from our homes. A few people knew that we were dating—his two elders, Deacon Anthony, Mom and Diana. The pastor had informed his mother and sister that we were seeing each other. We had planned to spend Thanksgiving with his family in the South.

I hadn't seen Darren in weeks and the calls had even stopped. Well, I did change my number, plus I was living with Mother until I could find what I wanted in the way of a large house, with a pool. In the weeks that I was seeing the pastor, Diana and I even attended Bible study, so I had grown spiritually. I was praying hard that my desires for the pastor would subside. It was so hard for me. I often wondered if it was hard for him, too.

As Diana and I tried to put the last box into my car, a white car pulled up and stopped. My gut instinct warned me that this was trouble. There were teenagers out playing basketball. They must have sensed trouble too because they stopped playing and began to walk rapidly toward us. A fair-skinned young woman with long curly hair jumped out of the car, waving a gun.

The box in my arms slammed to the ground and I turned to run. I screamed loud to my friend, "Diana, run!"

"I told you, bitch, I was going to kill you." This woman had a crazed look on her face. I even saw foam bubbling around her mouth. "Did you think I was kidding?" As we ran to the front door of the house, shots rang out.

Screaming at the top of her lungs, "Run, but trust me your ass is mine." *Pop, pop, pop.* "Take that, whores."

The sound was loud. She missed. As we ran toward the porch I turned to see how close the shooter was to us. It only took a minute to register who the lady was. As I turned to see her face I remembered her. She was the woman that I gave the directions to weeks ago at the service station.

I felt a sting in my arm. As I stared at the shooter, blood rushed over my hand. I was holding Diana screaming. She had fallen and I bent down to try to lift her up. She was no longer moving. I saw too much blood on her head. Thinking Diana was dead, I screamed an ear-deadening cry.

"I told you I was going to kill you! You took my man and now I'm taking your life! You just play with folks' feelings, but never again!"

She shot at me again. But she was a lousy shooter. She missed, but I fell backward to make her believe that she had shot me again. That act may have saved my life. When she pulled the trigger, the power of the gun thrust her backward and she fell to the ground. The woman took the gun and shot herself in the head. The teenagers rushed to help us. I had taken a bullet in my arm and Diana was bleeding from her head. When I turned back to see my friend, I lost my mind in anger and shock overcame me. Then I passed out.

I woke up a day later. I had had surgery to remove the

bullet from the upper part of my arm. My mother was there and so was the pastor, my sister and my brother. I tried to jump up, but my head hurt too much. When I passed out I hit my head hard on the ground. The teenagers used their cells to call 911. If they had not been there I could have bled to death.

As I looked up I saw everyone, but Diana. For a moment I didn't remember what had happened.

"Where is Diana? Please tell me she is all right. Please!" Lifting my head off the pillow again, I tried to sit up, but my head was throbbing. I lay back down.

My mother leaned down and told me that Diana was fine. A bullet had grazed the side of her head. Other than a deep cut that needed twenty stitches she was fine. When she fell, she knocked herself out. We were both going to be released after another day of tests and observations.

The pastor told me that the young woman had died. He explained that the woman was Darren's graduate assistant. Her name was Tammy and they had been having an affair for about six months when he broke it off. She was angry because she felt that I was in the way. Darren was not only two-timing his wife, but was doing the same thing to me. Tammy thought he loved her. She was the person who had burned his car. The police had found a notebook with incidents, places and things that she had done. Tammy was unstable. What Darren didn't know was that Tammy had been institutionalized in her teens for the same obsessive behavior over her high-school boyfriend. When Darren broke off their relationship, she stopped taking her medication. The police also told my mother and the pastor that Tammy left a suicide note, saying that she could not live through another relationship gone bad. Darren cooperated fully with the police and was not charged. After all, Tammy was twenty-one and old enough to know better. Well, that said, so was I. I knew that when the heart was involved, I would lose my ability to reason. I'd been in the same place, in love with a man who wasn't available for me. If the pastor had not shown an interest in me I might have been unable to let Darren go. But God knows our needs and He puts the right people in our lives at the right time, and for that I was blessed.

I felt bad for Tammy and Jill. Jill left Darren when she found out he was a repeat offender. She went through the blues with me, trying to hold onto her husband, but when she found out he was doing the same thing to me, she knew that he was a no-good user; a ladies' man who couldn't live without two or three women around. Unfortunately, the weakest one of us was not able to let him go and move on. Sadly, she took her own life rather than face life without the man she had grown to love. Tammy had worked side by side with Darren ever since her first year in college, only to begin a relationship with him during her last year. Darren would have to live with the guilt of dating such a troubled soul and hurting her.

The pastor said everyone was praying for us. "How do they know?"

"It made the news."

"Oh no." I started to cry. "Does everyone know my business?"

"The news reported a love triangle. But they said one of the victims had long been out of the picture." I held his hand. I didn't want to release it. I felt like my skeletons were exposed for the world to see. I didn't want him to hate me and I didn't want to lose him.

He bent down and kissed me on the lips as if he'd read my mind. "Nothing will pull me away from you." I thought about that. *Get out of my way, devil.*

I squeezed his hand again.

****

Once I was released from the hospital I began to have nightmares. I dreamed that Tammy was back repeatedly shooting at me and with every shot I passed out, only to wake up to find her shooting me again. I decided not to see the pastor as the inquest into Tammy's suicide was going on. I felt that too much had occurred and I didn't want him to end up in a scandal. He was sad, but did not pressure me.

I was still working with the youth in the church and they were now writing their thoughts in journals I had purchased and gave them. Some wrote beautiful poems. I attended church weekly and the pastor and I spoke, but stayed our distance. I was getting stronger in my beliefs. I loved God and believed He would deliver me.

I was in therapy and going to rehab to strengthen my arm. The worst part was wearing the cast and feeling all that itching that seemed hard to scratch. I was wearing a cast because the bullet had hit a bone. Other than the irritating itch, the nightmares and missing the pastor, I guess I was okay.

The women in the church were hot on the pastor's trail. They were some vicious women who were about to bite each other's head off if they thought the pastor was interested in someone other than them. I received four counseling sessions and was growing stronger. I decided to live the rest of the year out with my mother and brother. Terri had decided to move on campus to finish out her last year. For the Labor Day weekend the pastor was having a pool party. It was open to the church members, but about one-hundred people signed up to attend, as it was a holiday weekend.

The phone rang and I ran to pick it up. It was Diana.

"Hey, girl, how are you today?" Diana sounded chirpy.

"All is well I suppose."

"What do you mean? You don't sound so happy."

"The nightmares won't stop. Why am I having them and you are not?"

"That's a question for the doctor. However, remember you were being harassed, you were in a bad relationship, and you were close to the situation. Therefore, you would have the after effects more than I would. At least that is what I'm thinking. Can you imagine what happened to us, girl?

"I know. I cannot believe that women fall so hard they would kill and rather die than to live without a man. What's happening to us women? There was a time when men would beat and hurt us, threaten and stalk us to prevent us from leaving. When did women start that mess?

"I don't know, but I would think there are many women who do things like this, but they don't get discussed because it never reaches the level it did with you."

"I just want the dreams to go away."

****

We went to purchase some presentable bathing suits, as what we both had were way too sexy for a pastor's pool party. I found a black one-piece with lace in the middle. The back dipped all the way down to the top of my butt, but it was tasteful. Diana found a red one- piece in the same pattern. She had fallen hard for Deacon McKinley. I hoped he felt the same way. I did not want her heart to get broken as we had already experienced when her marriage dissolved because of another woman and with mine broken by a married man.

The weekend of the party, Diana and I discussed her growing relationship. She told me that the pastor missed me, but that she heard he had given up on me. "So what? I'm so over him, too."

Chapter 27

We arrived at the pool party at seven. It was a hot September evening. The party started at six, and was in full swing when we arrived. Only adults were present, as the youth department had a field trip planned to Memphis for camping. Plus, many of the teenagers had returned to college.

Diana found Deacon McKinley and I found my mother and her circle of friends. Occasionally, I would catch the pastor glimpsing at me, which bothered me since he had a woman attached to him like glue. I heard someone say she was from out of town and was the pastor's date. My heart ached, but I couldn't let on. I walked around, laughing and kidding with everyone. John Peters, a single church member, asked me to swim with him and I agreed.

The pastor's eyes were glued on me. He tried to turn his head, but as I dropped my wrap and he saw my sleek hourglass figure, I knew he still cared. I dived into the water and John came in after me.

"I'll race you to the other end," John said.

Before he could say another word I went under and swam underwater and then I came above and did the crawl to defeat him. I was faster due to spending four weeks in therapy for my arm and much of it was in the water. During my last doctor's visit the cast was removed. As my therapist said, water made my body lighter, thus making it easy for me to lift my stiff arm.

"Wow, Denise, you are a great swimmer."

"Thanks, John. I've had a lot of practice."

I stayed in the pool with John for more than an hour, swimming, racing and just talking. There were about thirty-five of us in the water. I noticed that the pastor was wearing some long shorts, a snug white T-shirt and flip-flops. As usual, he looked so sexy and I could barely keep my eyes off him. Plus, I was jealous that he decided to flaunt his new lady in my face. She was a tall, stunning lady who appeared in her late twenties or early thirties. She was stuck to his side like a Siamese twin. When I first noticed them, I asked Mother who she was and she said she wasn't sure and that she had never seen her before at the church or otherwise. It bothered me seeing him with another woman, even though I had stopped seeing him six weeks earlier.

John pulled me closer to him and whispered in my ear, "Are you dating anyone?"

"Yes."

"I'm certainly sorry to hear that." When he said that I turned to find the pastor and I saw the young lady hug him and they turned to walk into his house. For some reason, seeing them hug scared me and I panicked. I thought I had lost him forever.

"John, I'll be back." I jumped out of the pool, grabbed my wrap and walked toward the house in search of the pastor. I dried off my body and hair with a towel. As I walked toward the house I stopped to speak to several members, but I rushed to complete the conversations. I walked swiftly into the house. I saw him walk back into the front door of the house and the tears came. He was alone. When he looked up after locking the front door, our eyes met. He saw the tears and felt my pain. He rushed to me and I fell into his arms.

"Denise, what's wrong?"

"Hold me," I pleaded.

He pulled me tightly into his arms. "What's wrong?"

I couldn't talk. I was so ashamed. I was ashamed that it took me seeing him with another woman to decide that I needed and wanted him. I was so ashamed that I could not find the words to express my feelings.

"Come here." He pulled me into his study and locked the door. We were alone and we had privacy.

"Talk to me, baby."

I was speechless. But I clutched his head and pulled it toward me. Then I reached up and kissed him with everything in me. His lips welcomed mine. With our lips locked together I gripped his belt and tried to undo it. I released him and pulled the top of my swim suit down. My breasts were exposed. He kissed them, while I struggled to pull his pants down.

He grabbed my hands to stop me from exposing his penis. "Denise, stop! This is wrong."

"I need you. Please make love to me."

"No. Not now." He hurriedly pulled my swimsuit back up

and adjusted his pants while buckling his belt up. I stood there looking at him with my arms still wrapped around him. "Denise, I want you to stay until everyone leaves. The woman," he kissed me, "that you saw me with," he kissed me again, "is my cousin."

"I don't understand."

"You are the only one for me. Please know that! Stay after everyone is gone. Give me your car keys."

"I have to get them out of my purse."

He kissed my tear-stained face and embraced me. "We are going to be fine. She is my cousin. We haven't seen each other in a while. She ran interference for me by keeping the women at bay. You understand?"

I lifted my head to kiss him again and again. "I understand."

I went to retrieve my keys and gave them to James. We kissed again before I returned to the party. My attitude changed. I was now happier and friendlier. I spent the rest of the evening talking to the church members while James sat at a table, talking to the men of the church. Every now and then he stole a glance at me and I would do the same with him. I couldn't wait until everyone left. I needed to feel James' lips kissing mine. I needed to feel the softness caressing my lips, letting me know that he still cared. I wanted his arms to hold me.

The people finally started leaving around midnight. I was so happy, but knew that I needed to stay back without anyone noticing. I talked to Mother until she and her two church buddies were the last to leave. Diana and her date had left more than two hours earlier. I walked Mom to her car and continued to talk to her until the last car left. I told her that I would leave in a minute. She left and I walked back into the house. The pastor had already moved my car into his garage.

I walked through the door and Pastor Davis grabbed me and pulled me into his arms. He was kissing me so hungrily and passionately that I could barely catch my breath. As he kissed me, I leaned on the closed door and he locked it. As we kissed he untied my wrap and it fell to the floor. Next, he pulled the straps of my swimming suit down one by one until my breasts were showing. As he kissed me; he stripped me down to nothing. This was not the pastor I knew. He was a man who needed to be loved and held. We kissed until I pulled his T-shirt over his head and he dropped his pants. My eyes nearly bulged out of my head. He was gorgeous and everything I had ever dreamed of in a man.

We were naked as jaybirds. "Swim with me. I want to swim," he said.

He took my hand and we walked through the house to the backyard. The pastor's house sat on nearly three acres of land. His home and yard were protected by a tall privacy fence. We walked to the pool, admiring each other's bodies. I jumped in the pool and he came in after me. We raced to the other end. Once he caught me we kissed again. We swam to the lower end of the pool and he lifted me out of the water to sit me on the pool's ledge. Kissing my foot, he moved up to my leg, then my thighs until he tasted my center. After I reached my peak, he pulled my weakened body back into the water and entered me. "I love you, Denise."

"I love you." I kissed him all over his neck and face until we both were spent. Too weak to move we stood there in a tight hold for more than five minutes. Finally, we left the pool and went into the house. He wrapped me with a huge towel that he grabbed from the closet near the kitchen door. We were like giddy teens.

We found something to eat and sat around talking in our towels. After we drank some water he turned on the security system and took my hand. We walked upstairs to the second level to his bedroom where we made love until the wee hours of the morning. "Denise, that night you came into my bed, I wanted you so badly, but I couldn't take advantage of you. I am so sorry for hurting you that night. It wasn't that I didn't want to be with you, I was celibate until tonight. I have been celibate for seven years. I also fought hard not to commit fornication. I'm a pastor and I have to be stronger. I am so sorry; I couldn't fight my need for you tonight."

I reached up and kissed him. I didn't want to say anything to spoil how I was feeling. I was so ashamed about running to his bed that night I had that nightmare. I felt a little rejected, but since he held me that night in his arms I accepted the fact that we would not become lovers. Now that he explained why he refused my sexual advances, I understood. I fell asleep spooned into my lover.

I turned over bright and early the next morning, wanting to hold and kiss James, but he had already left the bed. Having no clothes to put on I remembered that I had a clean set of clothing in the car. So I went to find my keys and James. I didn't see him anywhere, but his car was still there. Not finding my car keys, I went into the garage, hoping he had disabled the house alarm and finding that he had, I entered the garage, opened the driver's door and pushed in the trunk button. I took out my exercise bag and seeing that the pastor's car was parked next to mine I went back inside to find him. Searching all the rooms, I pushed open a small door and found Pastor Davis, praying and crying. Careful so that he could not hear me, I backed out of the room and listened.

"Please forgive me, Father, for sinning. Lord, I get so weak with Denise. How can I stand in the pulpit and preach when I am fornicating? I'm so sorry, please forgive me. Please help me abstain from sex; strengthen me, Father. Please help me. I don't want to be lost, but I love her so much. Please, God, forgive me. Help me handle my feelings for her in a Christian way."

While standing there with tears rolling down my face, I realized the position I had put him in. I teased him most of the night in that little black bathing suit. Thinking he was with another woman, I nearly threw myself on him while trying to strip him naked and begging him to make love to me. He hadn't been with a woman sexually in seven years, I should have helped him, but I led him right where I wanted him, inside of me. Now he was hurting because he loved God just like I did, but he had God and an entire congregation looking up to him to be better than the people he was trying to bring to God.

I walked away, vowing to let him go. After I dressed and went back down to leave, I found him in the kitchen. "Hi, Pastor."

"Hi, Denise." He walked over and kissed my forehead. "You hungry?"

"No, I need to leave. Where are my keys?"

"You don't have to go."

"Yes, I do." I saw the keys hanging on a rack in the kitchen and I grabbed them and began to walk to the garage. "I'll see you later."

"Denise, talk to me."

"Nothing to say." I kissed him and he pulled me close and smelled my hair. "I love you."

"I'll call you," I said as I pulled away and walked through the door and got into my car. He pushed the garage pad and opened the garage. He blew me a kiss and said he would call me as I backed out and left. *I will not make anyone fall from the grace of God.* I promised myself that I would not see him again.

Chapter 28

"Denise, why won't you talk to the pastor? He keeps calling the house. What happened between you two?"

I didn't respond. He called me every day since the night I slept in his bed, but I refused to talk to him. All my life my mother said, "I hope I never cause anyone to stray from God." I believed that I had. I would not help the pastor lose sight of what God had planned for him. He was supposed to lead the sheep to righteousness, not astray. I even stopped going to church and was sulking.

"You and the pastor love each other and I am praying hard that you young folks get it right. You both need to stop fighting your love for each other."

I just sat there on the couch, ignoring my mother.

"Since you will not talk about him, Cynthia called this morning with an update on Sarah."

"She did? How is she doing in treatment?"

"She completed her twenty-eight day stay and moved to California. I am flying in the next two weeks to see her. I miss my friend."

"That's good, Mom. I'm glad that she is doing well."

"I wrote her letters during her stay, but she never responded."

"I can understand that, Mom; she had to concentrate on getting better."

"Well, I miss my friend. I hate that she did not allow me to go through this with her." Mom held her head down, so I wouldn't see the sadness in her eyes.

"Just know that she can only get better if she stays with her program." I caressed Mom's hand.

Smiling and feeling a little better, Mom refocused. "Back to you, young lady, you and the pastor really need to get this relationship thing you have together. Stop fighting it, Denise."

"I'm not fighting. It's just not meant to be." I crossed my leg.

"If you let what's supposed to happen, happen, it will."

"Well, Mom, there is no need in me seeing a pastor. Where is something like that going to lead to?"

"Hopefully, to the altar."

"See that's just it, I don't want to be a preacher's wife."

"You need to stop this nonsense and get off that couch and put on some clothes. You're just letting yourself go. When are you going back to work?"

"I don't know. I took a leave of absence."

"Well, if you don't love Pastor Davis, why did you leave your job?"

I grabbed the remote control to turn on the television. I was through with the conversation. Here I sat with a small hole in my arm where I took a bullet from a deranged woman over a man and I was not about to allow another man to break me down again. Did I love him? Yes, I did, with all my heart, but I never dreamed of being a preacher's wife. I couldn't see myself being a holy roller like that. I had seen too many folks walk around like they were closer to God than others. Not me, I was letting go now before things got a little too difficult.

As I sat on the couch, channel surfing, Diana called. "Happy Wednesday!" she screamed.

"Girl, you know you are a nut. Who calls people screaming 'Happy Wednesday? ' What's so happy about this Wednesday?"

"Tonight is Bible study. Please go with me. You haven't been in weeks."

"I don't feel like it. You have Deacon McKinley, so you'll be all right."

"Sweetie, it is you I am worried about. Don't pull away from the church and God because of what you are going through."

"I'm not doing that, Diana. I just don't feel like going."

"He loves you and you love him."

"Please stop! I don't want to deal with this now."

"Okay, your call. The teens have really been asking about you. They want to know when you are returning."

"Oh really?" I lifted myself up from the couch and started pacing back and forth with a huge smile on my face.

"Especially Trisha. She wants to see you. She's doing so well. She wants you to know how well she is doing in school. Plus, girl, even her appearance is changing. She's wearing nicer clothes and her hemline has been lower. You really worked with her."

"Well, I'm happy for her." I sat back on the couch, twisting my hair around my finger.

"Hello! Is anybody there?" Diana knocked on the phone's earpiece. "Come on, Denise. I want my friend back."

"I'm here. I just need some time." I rested my elbows on my thighs." I have been through so much. Maybe I need more counseling."

"Girl, you just need prayer. If God brought you to it, He'll bring you through it."

"Look at you. I bring you to church and now you all Ms. Holy Ghost."

"You got that right. But listen, girl, they are having a dating

game, something like a bid for a bachelor or bachelorette
in two weeks at church and they have asked that you
participate. They need more single, professional women who
can get the donations in. Since you won't come to church,
please come and help out the Women's Ministry. We need
you."

"I'll think about it."

"Okay. I'm going to put your name down. Since you don't
want the pastor, maybe you can find someone else."

"I don't want anyone else. I'll do it to take my mind off
him. Diana, I'll call you back. Mom just walked in to tell me I
have company now."

"Who is it?" Diana asked excitedly.

I didn't respond.

"It's the pastor, isn't it?"

"Yes, Diana. I'll talk to you later." I ended the call.

My mother let Pastor Davis in and allowed him to come
into the den where I was lounging and talking to Diana. I was
shocked to see him. As I hung up the phone, he looked me
in the eyes and asked, "Denise, what are you trying to do to
me?"

"I'm not trying to do anything to you."

"You are toying with my heart."

"I don't mean to. I'm sorry."

When he walked closer to me, I could tell he was hurting. It was all in his face. He had even lost weight. But I had decided that even though I loved him, his life was not what I wanted. I stepped back as he got nearer.

"Please stop running from me. I'm so tired." As I was about to say something, he grabbed me and pulled me close. We were staring into each other's eyes, not knowing what to do, and then suddenly he kissed me. My knees buckled and he pulled me back up to him. "Why can't you just love me?" he asked with such sincerity it hurt me.

"I can't. I just want to be friends."

"Friends? Is that what you want? Your kisses say you want more. Your body says you want more. Is that all you can say to me when I want you to be my wife?"

I pulled away.

"Denise, if you push me away this time I am not coming back. I am not to be played with. I have put everything on the line with you—my ministry, my life. I love you with everything in me and if you don't want that from me just say it. But when I walk away this time, I'm not coming back."

We stared as if we were in a duel. *The first one to speak would lose.* I didn't want to speak. I was fearful of what would come out of my mouth. *I'm not playing. I want him out of my life.*

"Denise, what do you want? Do you love me?"

I stared, but didn't speak. He finally kissed me with everything in him. When he let me go he smelled my hair and kissed me all over my face and neck. "I'd love you forever if you let me."

He walked out, leaving me standing looking and feeling stupid. I had just lost the man of my dreams. I thought I loved Darren, but that was before I experienced a pure earnest love from James. Why I didn't want to be with him when I truly loved him was beyond me. Was the devil interfering? If I gave in, I would be converted. If I stayed away from him and the church I would still be outside the church, looking in and running back when I needed God to lift me out of my pain again. But I wouldn't run. Without him I would work hard to be a Christian. I was going to participate in the dating game while praying to God to show me the way to His Kingdom and if it was His will for the pastor to be the man He planned for me, I would obey. I needed God to help me because Satan was pulling me away from the church. I hadn't stepped foot in the church in weeks. It was time to go back.

Chapter 29

Three days after I saw the pastor, the church board called an emergency meeting. Diana called to tell me that the pastor had stepped down.

"What do you mean he stepped down?"

"He submitted a letter of resignation, but they asked him to reconsider and to take a leave of absence. Denise, you are destroying him. You love him, but you don't want his life like this, right?" Diana blew air into the phone.

"I know it's stupid. Let me work this out."

I hung up the phone and went down on my knees. "Please, God, help me to make the right decision. I really do love James. Please don't let him give up what he was called to do. Only you know his heart. Please help us to live according to Your will. Please bless him. I love him. You know my heart. I need you to help guide us. When I am with him, I put him in a position that causes him to go against Your will. I don't want to be the cause of his downfall. Please help me to love him the way he needs to be loved."

I spent the rest of the week in tears. I was so troubled. I decided to go to church and participate in the dating game. I was not planning on going on the date, but would help them raise money. I would be clear with whoever chose me that I wasn't interested in them, but had participated to raise funds.

On Sabbath I arrived at the church near the eleven o'clock hour. The first person I saw was Sister Clay. It had been a while since I had seen or shared words with her.

"I see you did it, huh? You broke that man down. I knew he would not stay in the pulpit after seeing a sinner like you."

I kept walking, but she walked up on me.
"What did the pastor see in you? You are a tramp."

I turned to smack the heck out of her, but Deacon McKinley and Diana grabbed my hand and pulled it back. "Don't stoop down to her level," Diana warned.

"*Her level*? What do you mean? Because your friend is a tramp? She knew what she was doing with the pastor. Shame pulled him out of the pulpit. The devil sent you here to destroy this church."

I walked up to Sister Clay and whispered, "You are a poor, sick, confused and misguided soul. Satan is your only friend and even he is sick of you."

I walked away because a crowd had started to gather around us, but I wasn't going to give Sister Clay the satisfaction of having an audience for her nonsense. I went into the church and listened to Elder Bryant preach. He had agreed to take over until the pastor returned.

After church was over I met with the Women's Ministry team and the other women church members who would participate. The men involved were a secret. We wouldn't find out until we chose our dates. The activity was scheduled for the following week. They had already sold five-thousand dollars in tickets. I spent the entire week thinking and praying and reading the Bible. Several times I picked up the phone to call Pastor Davis. Diana told me that the elders and deacon had rallied around the pastor.

The night of the activity I decided to wear my black, off-the-shoulder stretch rayon dress. Since we were trying to raise money I wanted to look great, but tasteful. So even though the dress was fitting and showed my shape, it covered my body except the top of the shoulders. As I dressed and primped to leave the house, I wondered which men would participate.

When I arrived at the church the parking lot was packed. The activity was being held in the huge church fellowship hall. They wanted to raise money, not spend it, so the team decided to use the fellowship room, which seated three-hundred people. It had a nice stage that could be extended into the audience. Women and men were everywhere. I searched for my mother and Diana. They were sitting at a center table. As I walked toward them I felt like all eyes were on me. The men stared at me hungrily while the women stared at me with envy.

"Hi, Mom." I bent down to kiss her and kissed Diana on the cheek.

"Hi, baby, you look so beautiful." Momma beamed with pride.

"Thanks, Momma." I sat in the chair between Momma and Diana. Diana leaned over and whispered into my ear, "I haven't seen the Pastor."

"I didn't ask if you did."

"Don't play. That dress is for him. You look absolutely gorgeous."

I smiled. As I turned to say something else, the program coordinator announced that the program was about to start.

"Ladies and gentlemen, we, the Women of the Shiloh Seventh Day Adventist Church, would like to welcome each of you to our Bid for Single Christians fundraiser. Please know that we are raising money for our church and scholarship programs. Every person who agreed to participate in this activity completed a questionnaire and a personal interview. In addition, everyone who is participating has been a member in good standing of the church or has been referred by someone in the church. So these people are business folks; Christian people who love God. All right, Saints. Let's get this show on the road. I now introduce to you our Mistress of Ceremony, Sister KC Stevens."

As the Program Coordinator read off the credentials of KC Stevens, several women and men were asked to go to the stage area. I would be auctioned near the end. The group settled for a dinner and auction. It would all be in good taste. No waving of money, no screaming and clowning, only waving a finger to show that they were bidding.

The first lady, a schoolteacher, who was a sweet person in her late thirties, was auctioned off to a deacon for $1000 dollars. Deacon Patrick was not going to give up. He had had his eyes on Pricilla Jemison for a long time and had made up his mind that he did not care what it cost; he would win a date with her.

Next up was a preacher from St. Louis. Outside of being a dynamite preacher with a huge following he was also an accountant with his own company. A bachelor who was dating, but looking for a wife, the women's ministry team convinced him to participate. He finally was sold to the successful and sexy, Thelma Bennett, city administrator for Belleville, Illinois. She out bid all the women in the Christian community and paid $3,800 for a date with the dapper minister. As more women were presented, the total amount of money increased rapidly.

So far the total raised was over $22,000. As I searched the room for the pastor and did not see him, I turned and whispered to Diana, "I can't believe he would miss this activity."

"When people are hurting, this means nothing. Who feels like pretending to have fun when their heart is aching." Diana hunched her shoulders like I was supposed to understand that crap she was saying.

I was the eighth person to be auctioned out of ten. As I walked to the stage to take my place, no one would have anticipated what was about to happen. Once some of the more wealthy men in the church community found out I would be in the auction, they were ready to get a date with me. I was professional and admired by many, at least until the sordid details came out about the shooting and the affair. Until that time I had a clean reputation. Mother said that I was marriage material. I guess that meant that I was independent, educated, could hold a conversation with anybody and run a household while maintaining a business.

As I walked across the stage, the Mistress of Ceremony

read off my profile. As the auctioneer began the bid at $100, before she could blink the bid was at $500, then $1,000. Suddenly, someone in the corner said $2000 and it was on. Another man said $2,500, then $3,000. Before I knew it my bid was at $6,000. Two pursuers began walking toward the stage in a bidding duel. I turned to look at who the bidders were and was shocked to see Pastor Reynolds from the Sunny Shore Church in St. Louis, with a membership of 10,000. He was a widower who had lost his wife more than three years earlier. He was forty and I could not have imagined why he was bidding for me. I didn't know him and prior to this evening had never met him. Pastor Davis was the other bidder walking toward the stage; he looked at me with determination, and said, 'Ten-thousand dollars." There was a loud hiss in the room and people were getting louder. I looked at him and my heart fluttered. I could not hold back my smile. I loved him and I knew it deep down. I was shocked that he would publicly pursue me at the auction."

The auctioneer said, "Ten thousand going once, twice, sold to the gentleman on the right." With that, Pastor Davis grabbed my hand and led me off the stage. As the noise rose to a high level the auctioneer asked everyone to please be seated and allow the last two people to finish out the program.

The pastor held my hand as we exited the building. He saw Deacon Bryant and asked me for my car keys. I looked into my purse and handed them to him. He walked over and handed the keys to the deacon. He asked the deacon to take care of my car. We got into his black Mercedes and he pulled off the lot. I didn't ask any questions. He didn't say anything. For a man to pay $10,000 for one date, I knew that this was serious and I was going to allow whatever was going to happen, happen. I was tired. I had no more fight in me. I just never in a million years thought that I would be head over heels about a minister.

He drove without speaking. The car was quiet. Not scary, or nothing to make me nervous, but just quiet. I didn't know what to anticipate. He pulled into his driveway and opened the garage. Driving into the garage, he shut the motor off and hit the button in his car to close the garage door. Then he walked over to my side and helped me out of the car. We entered the hallway and he turned and kissed me so passionately that I almost lost my balance. Taking my hand, we walked into his dining area. Jazz music was playing. He took me in his arms again and kissed me. Then he pulled out the chair at the table for me to be seated. Soon, two waiters walked in, carrying trays and plates. We were served pasta with broccoli, sweet carrots and Spinach Quiche. Since I arrived late to the auction I didn't eat. We both ate small servings, but still did not say much. After cheesecake with strawberry topping, he took me by the hand and we walked out back. As we walked, starring at the moon, he turned, kissed me, bent down to his knee and reach into his pocket. My poor heart was pounding so hard, it felt as if it was about to explode in my chest.

"Denise, you know how much I love you."

I just stared down into his eyes. My hands were shaking and my left leg was bouncing out of control.

"Yes, I know."

"Will you marry me?"

"Yes, I will. I love you, James."

He stood and slid a beautiful diamond band on my finger. Most Seventh Day Adventists don't wear jewelry. For them it is about putting things and obsessions before God. The women in some churches wear wedding bands. He stood, pulled me close and kissed me again. When we walked back into the house, he checked to make sure that the help was gone and then he locked and secured his house. I stopped and pulled off my black dress sandals. He held my hand to steady me. Then he swooped me into his arms, kissed me passionately and carried me to his bed. He didn't stop loving me until I stopped screaming and crying from his touching, kissing and sucking.

After my third orgasm he said that he had a private jet ready to take us to Vegas and asked if I would leave with him in the morning to get married.

"Yes. But I don't have a change of clothes."

"Don't worry! I had a personal shopper buy you several complete outfits and we can shop in Vegas." I held him firmly and kissed him over and over. Finally, we both slipped into a beautiful restful sleep.

Chapter 30

Sunday, November 18, I woke up to the smell of peach tea percolating in the tea kettle. I slid Pastor's large T-shirt that he had laid on the bed over my head and walked downstairs. He was standing at the stove, scrambling eggs. I stood there, watching him. He was absolutely gorgeous. From the back I could see his muscles protruding from his black T-shirt. His waistline seemed to have been personally sculpted by God. I wondered why women in his congregation were not able to snag him. Then it occurred to me that maybe he didn't want women going against each other, or dissension in his church, or even still, gossiping over his love life. But had he dated someone at the church I may never have met him nor had an opportunity to have a second chance at love. I smiled to the heavens. *Thank you, God, for blessing us.*

Pastor turned and smiled at me. With the skillet in his hand, he walked toward me and kissed me.

"Good morning, beautiful."

"Good morning." I smiled with all thirty-two teeth showing. "Let's have breakfast, shower and then we can leave by twelve o'clock." He grabbed my hand and sat me in front of the plate he prepared for me. Bending down, he kissed me, slipping his tongue into my month and lightly sucking mine. After breakfast we made love, showered, dressed and waited on the limousine to arrive to take us to the airfield. By one-thirty we were in the beautiful blue skies, headed to Las Vegas. We were in a private jet. It was not his, but an old friend's. We talked, kissed and hugged until I found myself sound asleep in the big plush leather seats. When I felt his lips on mine we had landed. A limo driver was waiting for us, holding up a sign for the Davis family. We walked over and James talked to the driver. Soon we were headed for Mandalay Bay. Mandalay Bay Resort and Casino was set at the south end of the strip and served as a charming escape from boredom; the luxury resort had lots of elegance and excitement in its restaurants, entertainment and sun-drenched beach. We were booked to stay in the Executive King Suite.

"How long are we here?" I wanted to know so that I could call the office and let them know my return date.

"Five days. Then hopefully we can return, handle some business items and leave for Hawaii. I want to travel with you, so that we can get to know each other in every way. Do you have a problem with that?"

"No." I said, squeezing his hand.

This was my first time in Vegas. It looked like a tourist town to me with hotels everywhere. People were walking around and I could tell that they were visiting as they looked upward to view the tall hotels and other attractions. As the limo driver cruised down Las Vegas Boulevard, I thought about how I had fallen in love with the man next to me, tenderly holding my hand. It was no easy task. I had been through so much since I had met him. He was still in love with me even after I dated a married man, had been shot and rejected him. It was now evident that God could change people, even people like me.

I started studying my Bible all the time. Each day I was becoming more spiritual and leaned more on God. It was HE who brought me through when I was feeling so lost. God was there when I was shot and so many other times. I could not begin to count the ways and the many times that God answered my prayers and saved my life. I had resolved that I would not bring a pastor down with sex. I knew that he was a man, not perfect like God, but I continued to pray that God would forgive both of us as He did Peter.

"I love you so much, Denise. I have always loved you from the moment our eyes met."

"No, that is impossible."

"Why is that so impossible?"

"I was not a Christian. Why would you love me out of all the women in the church?"

"God can change anyone. We don't pick who we fall in love with. Most of the time God does. Sometimes though, people don't heed His advice. That's why so many people fail to stay married. They don't ask God to help them to find the one."

"Did you ask Him?"

"You know I did. That's why when you walked through the door I knew."

I reached over and pulled him closer. "I love you so much." At that moment we both agreed to abstain from sex until we were officially man and wife. We also agreed to get baptized together and that James would not preach again until he did so.

After checking in, we kissed and walked over to the

elevators. As we waited, we kissed. Out of the side of my peripheral view, I saw a flash. Thinking nothing of it, I kept kissing the pastor. Once the doors of the elevator opened, we walked on. Suddenly, reaching out he grabbed me with urgency and pulled me into his body. He kissed me on the neck, face and nuzzled my breasts. *Flash! Flash!* There it was again. I pulled away and saw a tourist snapping pictures of us.

I could not tell who it was because the person had on a large hat, and the camera lens was covering her eyes.

"Did you see that woman in front of the elevator?"

"What woman?"

"The one who was snapping pictures."

"No, I didn't see anyone because I was too busy kissing the woman I love."

I bent down and kissed his lips. I love this man so much and to think I almost gave up this kind of love for a fool.

We walked into our room. I checked out the entire suite. It was gorgeous. I ran over to the room and looked out the large paneled window. I could see the boulevard and all the hotels with their glaring and beautiful lights and structures.

"Come here, baby." I pulled him toward the window. "Look how beautiful our scenery is."

"Not as beautiful as you though." I smiled so hard my

cheeks burned with desire.

Chapter 31

We enjoyed the rest of the day after we changed our clothes. We walked through the hotel to see its offerings. We went to the Mandalay Beach, though I had on some white cotton comfortable short pants that were not too short and not too long. James wore some khaki knee shorts and sandals with a striped shirt. He looked so sexy to me.

We strolled on the beach, taking in the sights and walked to the wave pool, the lazy river and the three swimming pools. It was so relaxing. We stayed out, people watching and walked back to the hotel, which was easy to do because the hotel provided quick access to the beach area. After we went back through the hotel we decided to visit the aquarium to watch the different types of fish. All and all we had a pretty peaceful afternoon. When we walked out of the aquarium, located at the bottom of the hotel, James leaned over and French-kissed me. When we pulled away, I was blinded again by a flash. I reached up as if my hand was a sunvisor to block out the lights; I could barely see from the bright flash.

"Baby, someone is taking pictures of us."

James wrapped his arms around me and kissed me again. "They are snapping pictures because you are gorgeous."

I could not hide my smile. I knew that if people looked at me right at that second, they would see that my face had turned a couple of shades darker. Blushing hard from his compliment, I took my fingers and lifted his chin up and kissed him several times. *I am so blessed to have this handsome man who loves me.*

We walked through Mandalay Bay's gift shop and purchased souvenirs. James could not keep his lips off me. He kept putting his hand through my hair and kissing me at the elevator as we went back to the room. The whole time we kissed I had an eerie feeling we were being watched.

Many people go to Vegas to have a quickie marriage. The chapel I had heard the most about was The Little White Chapel. It was the one that James chose for us. It was quaint.

I wasn't surprised when we returned to the room and I found three white wedding dresses lying on the bed. The most beautiful one was an asymmetrically draped strapless stretch Mikado Mermaid gown with a full organza skirt with ladder techniques. With my body shaped like an hour glass I felt it would be the best dress for me. James had gone into another suite with his best friend and I was awaiting Diana who had arrived that morning with her finance', Deacon Anthony McKinley. I sat on the bed and thought about my life. *Not too long ago, I was so in love with a married man. I never thought I could love anyone as much as I loved Darren. But it goes to show that God always comes through and when He does He shows out. Look at me now.*

As I reflected on my life, I heard knocking on my door. I got up and let Diana in. Her mere presence made my heart shout with happiness. I cuddled her.

"Can you believe this? I am getting married!"

We both began jumping up and down like teenagers. Excitement filled our hearts and the room.

"Let me see the dress. James told us he had picked some

out for you."

"I picked this one." I put the dress up against my body and tried to spin around so she could get a good view, but the train was a little cumbersome.

"That dress is so you. You are going to be a beautiful bride." Diana had tears building up in her eyes and they were threatening to fall.

"Don't start crying, girl." I took her hand and we sat down. "I want you to know that you are the best friend that everyone should have. I love you so much and I am so thankful and so blessed that God spared our lives so that we could live to see this day happening. Diana, God works in mysterious ways. It's hard to believe that I was in love with another man less than five months ago."

"I know. God has a way of leading us to our destiny if we allow Him to. Pastor James is a great catch, a good preacher and teacher. I pray he returns to the pulpit."

"You don't have to worry about that. James and I have decided to recommit our lives to God. As a matter of fact, when we return, we are going to get baptized together. We sinned, but we are asking God every day to forgive us. We know God has. In two days I will be his wife."

"Diana we're both getting married. I knew Deacon was gonna ask you to be his wife. I'm so happy for you." We stood holding hands.

"Did you ever think I would be remarrying?"

"Are you kidding me, girl? Yes! You are so beautiful,

successful and smart. We both found love in God's house."

"Thank you, Jesus!" We both said the words at the same time and burst out laughing.

We talked until it was dinner time and James, Anthony, Diana and I went to dinner. It was so beautiful and peaceful. When we returned to the room, James said he would be sleeping in the adjoining room. He wanted our wedding day to be special. Plus, we prayed earlier that day and asked God to forgive us for not abstaining and then made a commitment to not make love again until we were officially married. Before he left, I walked over to the large paneled window and stared at the city. I was quiet. James walked over. "Are you okay?"

"Yes. I'm happy, that's all."

"Come here." James pulled me into his arms and kissed my neck. "We are so blessed. You know that, right?"

"Yes, I do." I kissed him. "I was praying and thanking God for saving me from that bullet and from all the pain I'd been through. I thanked Him for keeping your mind and thoughts on me."

"That wasn't hard to do. I loved you from day one."

We kissed again. His lips were so soft. "Baby, let's go to bed before we break our vow to God again." Even though earlier that morning we became so passionate with each other, but since arriving we had not been intimate except for that one uncontrollable moment in the elevator when we first arrived and James kissed me all over my cleavage in the elevator.

That's when I first noticed the flash.

We toured Vegas. We went to the other hotels and rode the tram. We bought gifts for each other. We looked at the gambling areas, but did not partake. We ate at the restaurants, visited the beach and prepared ourselves for the big day, trying to make sure that we also had time to rest. On the way back to the hotel late Tuesday, I saw the back of a woman who reminded me of someone.

I pointed to the woman. "James, doesn't the back of that woman look like Sister Clay?"

Laughing he asked, "Now, sweetheart, how would I know how the back of Sister Clay looks?"

I laughed.

We went to dinner with our friends and returned to rest for our big day. That night I dreamed that James was asked to give up his church membership. I woke up sweating and crying. I jumped up and started praying. "Dear God, please take care of James. Please strengthen him spiritually and bless him so that he will continue to do Your work. He is a good, dedicated and loyal Christian. I know that we are not perfect, so I ask that you forgive James and I for allowing our passion and love to make him stray from doing Your will. We give our hearts to You, Lord, because we love You. Keep us in Your Word and be with us tonight and tomorrow as we dedicate our lives to You. Remove these bad thoughts from my mind and bless my family, friends and loved ones."

****

I woke up bright and early. The sun was blaring down on the large picture window. Although the sunbeams were loud and glowing I was so excited. This was the day most women dreamed about. I always wanted to walk down the aisle to meet my handsome husband. I believed it would be Darren. We never know what God has planned for our lives. In the last eight months, I experienced so much turmoil. I experienced a broken heart, almost lost my life and fell in love again in a short period of time. My mother always told me that our time was not God's time. What might be to Him a thousand years could be one year for us. I understood exactly what she was saying. People say God works in mysterious ways, but the truth is, God knows our needs and desires and in His time He will grant us what we ask for. But most of the time we are too impatient to wait on God, thus we pick the wrong people to be in our lives.

I was so happy that as I showered, the tears ran down my face, mixing in with the water. They were not tears of sorrow, but tears of joy. I missed Mom, Terri and my brother, Don. I wished they could be there with me. I cried because on this important day I should've been standing with family, but I was happy because I had James, Diana and most of all, God.

I exited the shower, grabbed my towel and dried off my body. I used my favorite body and bath moisturizer and lotion to smooth over my skin. The lotion, Twilight Woods, smelled so good that it soothed the sadness that tried to overtake me. As I put on my undergarments and robe I silently prayed. "Lord, my family is not with me today to witness this joy that You have provided me with, but I am thankful that You promised to never leave me. Thank You, God, for all the blessings that You have given me. I worship You, Lord, and I love You."

After praying I felt a cool breeze whisk across my face. I did not know where it came from, but I knew with everything in me that it was God letting me know that He was there with me as He had always been. Feeling a smile stretch across my face, I felt a sudden joy. Just as quickly, a loud thunderous knock shook the door. I jumped up and ran to answer it. I slung the door open.

"Diana, what took you so lon—?" I could not get the words out because I was shocked to my core. "Darren," I said with a calmness that flowed through my body. He was holding a big black shiny gun.

Chapter 32

"Hi, Darren, please come in." I pulled the door open so that he could maneuver himself in. As I stepped to the side to allow him to pass, I noticed that he was sweating profusely. Yet I was not afraid. I knew that God was with me. Had I moved too suddenly to slam the door the gun could have possibly gone off.

"What are you doing, Darren? This is not you? How did you find me?"

He walked in. His hands were shaking. "I'm so confused. I hate you, Denise, and if I can't have you no one will."

"Darren, you are hurting," I said calmly as I reached out my hand to him. He was about to lower the gun, but as if someone urged him to stay on target, he pointed it back straight at my heart.

"I lost everything because of you. You can't live to be happy when I am so miserable."

"You may have lost everything, but you can find happiness again. With God, everything is possible. Don't let Satan take more from you." I kept my voice at a low soft level.

"Whether you know it or not, your family needs you. They could not handle losing you. Remember, your wife fought for you."

I turned my back to him and walked into the sitting area of my room. He followed me, but he was silent.

"Darren, how did you find me?"

"I have been following you for weeks. I kinda figured you were coming here to get married. It was so easy to track you."

"You didn't love me. If you did, it would have only been me, not Tammy and your wife. If you really loved me I would have been enough. Sometimes, the devil makes you do things you would never normally do. Tammy and I were the distractions the devil provided to hurt you and break up your home, but you can find happiness again."

"How?" He lowered the gun. "I'm hurting so badly."

I reached over to touch his hand. "Darren, may I pray with you? God can fix everything. Maybe you can visit with your children and work on building a relationship with them. Do you love your wife?"

"Yes, I do, with all my heart."

"Tell her, but more than anything show her. Go to God and dedicate your life to Him and ask Him to give you your family back. Matthew chapter seven, verse seven, states: *Ask, and it shall be given to you; seek, and ye shall find; knock, and it shall be opened unto you.* If you have faith, even small like a mustard seed, God will give you the desires of your heart."

"Denise, I am so sorry. Please forgive me for coming here to hurt you. I'm so sorry." Darren laid the gun on the couch, bowed his head and just cried. "Please forgive me for everything." He wiped his eyes as I stood up and walked over to him. I took his hand and asked him to kneel. He and I both kneeled and bowed our heads. "Heavenly Father, I come to You today to ask You to help my friend. His heart is broken and he feels so lost without You. But You said that You would give us the desires of our hearts if we ask. I am asking You to take care of Darren and bless him. Help him and his family to reunite. Give him the courage and the wisdom to get his family back. Help him to understand that without You, he nor I could do anything. Lord, please bless and take care of my friend and help him to stop hurting. Help him to find peace. I know with You all is possible." Before I could end the prayer, Darren started praying.

"Father, I am so sorry for all the pain I have caused with my philandering ways. Help me to be happy and satisfied with the life and family You have provided me with. Help Jill to forgive me and to attend counseling so that we can save our marriage. Bless Denise and her soon-to-be husband. Thank You, Lord, for stopping me from totally ruining my life. Thank You, Lord, and thank you, Denise for not having me arrested." We both cried in each other's arm.

As we stood I hugged him again. "How did you get here?"

"I drove here, but I flew in from St. Louis."

"Where did you get the gun?"

"My cousin."

"Give me his number and I will call him to pick it up."

Darren gave me the number and I called his cousin and explained to him what was going on and that he needed to come to the Mandalay Bay Hotel and pick up Darren and his gun. While I was on the phone, someone knocked on the door.

"Darren, I'll get that," I said as I hung the phone up.

I opened the door, and Diana walked in, but stopped dead in her tracks when she spotted Darren. "Darren, what are you doing here?"

"Diana, everything is fine. He was just leaving." I turned back to Darren, "Darren, wait downstairs for your cousin and when he arrives I will bring the package down, okay?"

"Okay, Denise. Thank you so much for everything. Thank you."

"Be blessed, brother, and remember to seek God and all else will be okay."

He bent down and kissed my left cheek. He walked out the door with his head held higher than it was when he walked in. I shut the door and walked over to the couch and gently picked up the gun. Finding my makeup case, I emptied my products on the dresser and put the gun in and zipped the bag. While I was doing this, Diana's lip was hanging to the floor. "Close your mouth, Diana. Everything is fine. I'll tell you everything. But right now we need to get ready.

Diana helped me get ready. When I looked into the mirror I started crying. "Thank you, God, for sparing my life again. You are so merciful. I knew You were here with me. I felt Your presence. Thank You, Lord. I'm so happy. Thank You for having my best friend here with me. Bless my marriage and help me to live for You."

Diana reached up and wiped my tears with a Kleenex. "Sweetheart, you are messing up your makeup. Let me dry your face." After wiping my face, she stepped back and admired me. "You look absolutely stunning." The phone rang and Diana picked it up.

Passing the phone to me I said, "Hello?" The voice on the other end revealed itself to be Darren's cousin. I explained to the caller that my best friend would bring the gun down and told him what she was wearing. 'Take care of Darren."

As I hung the phone up, Diana shook her head. "You have some explaining to do. I'll call you to let you know that Darren is out of the hotel.

Chapter 33

God works in mysterious ways. Yes, I knew what that meant. In saving me, God was saving Darren, too. We both had to ask God to forgive us in order to go on with our lives. Darren lost his job due to fraternizing at work with a subordinate, but he didn't lose his credentials because the student was a consenting adult. He would find another job, because if he stayed with God, God would provide.

As I rode the elevator down to the waiting limousine, I felt so peaceful and so happy. I realized that none of us knew the paths our lives would take. I never dreamed that I would marry a preacher, get shot, have a gun pulled on me while being so calm, but I knew that the presence of the Lord was near.

As I walked through the hotel, people stared and mouthed, "She is so beautiful." I felt more than beautiful. I felt blessed.

Diana and I rode in the limousine to the Little White Chapel and as I exited out of the car, and walked through the door, I noticed the room had about ten people waiting around. "Diana, who are these people? I hope we are not interrupting another wedding."

Diana escorted me to the side and when I turned around, I screamed, "Momma!"

"Oh, baby, you look absolutely amazing." She kissed both of my cheeks. "I am so happy for you. You are a beautiful bride and I want you to remember to always let God direct your path."

"Thank you, Momma, for being here. I love you. You have been such a wonderful mom."

"Dry your tears, girl, and let's marry this man before someone else snatches him up."

The music started playing and Diana pulled my veil down. Then she walked in. As the bridal music played I was escorted by my brother, Don, who had surprised me, too. As I moved down the aisle to the man of my dreams, I passed Ms. Sarah and her daughter, James' mother and sister, my sister, Terri, Elder Bryant and Elder Grant.

I was so proud of Sarah. She had gone through treatment twice, had been clean and sober for four months and was happy to be with her daughter and grandchildren. Plus, she sold her house and Momma was going to visit her again in her new place in California. What could be better than having everyone I loved there with me for this joyous occasion?

As I took my place next to James, he could not stop smiling. *Thank You, Lord* was all I could think as we said "I do" and sealed it with a kiss. *Thank You, Lord, for directing my steps and hearing a sinner's cry.*

Epilogue

James and I shared an amazing week in Las Vegas. I could not have asked for a better and more caring husband. We left Vegas on the following Wednesday and spent two days moving some of my things to his home. We agreed to stay there because I absolutely loved it. Friday night as I lay in his arms, his cell phone buzzed. He picked it up and jumped straight out of bed.

"What's wrong, honey?"

"Go back to bed."

I got out of bed and walked up to him." "We are not going to start our marriage like this. We agreed to discuss everything involving our lives. If it is a member who is in need of counseling, that's different. But you are my husband and I want you to trust me."

"I'm sorry, baby. I just don't want you to be hurt. You are going to be tested and tried and you are going to have to find strength in me and God to deal with church issues."

"I know that."

"Come here, sweetheart." I leaned into him and he showed me his cell. I looked at the face of it and saw James and me in the elevator at Mandalay Bay with his face buried in my chest, kissing me in the cleavage area. It shocked me, but seeing the picture almost made me laugh.

"I told you I kept seeing a flash in Vegas. Someone was following us and taking pictures."

"I'm gonna speak to Darren."

"I know you think it was him because he followed us there, but if you had been there to see how God was working with Darren you wouldn't believe it was him. Like I said, honey, Darren was distraught and confused, bringing a gun to shoot me, but I know that God was working with him. If he took that picture he wouldn't have cried and asked God to forgive him. You had to be there to hear him praying to God."

"I still can't believe that brother pulled a gun on you. I don't know what I would have done if I had walked into that room and saw him pointing a gun at you. I would have beaten his butt and probably killed him myself."

"That's exactly why God made sure you were nowhere near. Being a murderer and locked up was not the plan God had for you nor was taking Darren's freedom. God needs more men in the vineyard."

"I know God chose you for me and He could not have picked a better helpmate."

The phone rang and it was Elder Bryant. He told James that a special meeting was being called at church. The board wanted to discuss the picture that was being texted throughout the church congregation.

If we had not had God in our lives we would have been hurt, but because we had asked God to forgive us and had gotten married we had no guilt or shame. James kissed me. "We'll be all right. Like everything else, we'll handle this, too."

****

James met with the board when we got back and explained that he and I were married in Vegas. He furthered explained that God had forgiven him, that he knew from the moment he met me that God had answered his prayers. With that, the board was impressed and understood that Pastor James was just a man, not a perfect man, but a mere human, just like them. They asked him to return to the pulpit once he recommitted himself to God. He agreed to do that, but in the meantime we would announce our marriage in church to the members the following Sabbath.

It was a long week. Hearing so much gossip about the no-good pastor who was having sex with the church tramp could have been too much for a new Christian, but James' and my love was so strong that it stood the test of time.

Sabbath morning, James and I attended morning service. The church was jam packed. I figured members who hadn't been there in a while showed up expecting a show and a lot of drama, but we would not give them that satisfaction.

After the praise singers sang and the prayers were prayed, Elder Bryant called James and me to the front of the church. As we left our seats and walked hand in hand to the pulpit, all eyes were on us. I felt confident and strong. I felt the presence of the Lord in the house. Satan was not going to tear God's house down.

Elder Bryant hugged us both. "Church, we have been through so much in the last week. Someone has allowed Satan to use them to try to hurt our pastor and Sister Denise Reese. But our God is a mighty God, and what He has built, no man can destroy, unless He allows it. Unfortunately, for the person who sent that picture of Pastor James and Denise out to harm them, you just introduced them earlier than we had planned. Members, friends and laymen, please allow me to introduce you to Pastor and First Lady James Davis. "

There was a loud commotion. People started whispering. "Order please," Elder Bryant requested. "Congregation, our dear pastor was married in Vegas and we are here to welcome him and his bride to us as the new First Lady of Shiloh Seventh Day Adventist Church. They will also be a part of the baptismal ceremony this evening. Furthermore, whoever sent that picture is welcome to cleanse their soul by joining the candidates for baptism. Remember, God hears every sinner's cry."

"Oh hell nawh!" screamed Ms. Clay. "This is a travesty."

"Sit your butt down woman or leave," Brother Johnson, the church screamer, said as he stood up. "You need to stop all that gossiping and destruction or you are going to bust hell wide open with that mess."

Trisha, who had rescheduled her baptismal and was now going to be baptized with us stood up. "Sister Clay, you really need to join the baptism tonight, because you need to release those demons."

Sister Clay turned her head in slow motion toward Trisha. She swung her head around and her eyes looked small, red and beady. She hissed at Trisha. "You want to be a Christian? Stay in your ghetto lane. This is not the end of this." Sister Clay rushed out of the church, pushing members out of her way. As she sulked and hissed while walking out, the members stood and clapped.

Elder Bryant looked sad and embarrassed. "Church, let's pray. Satan will never win." He prayed for Sister Clay, the pastor, me and the congregation. Then he asked the congregation to welcome the newly married First Couple.

The pastor and I walked back into the congregation and the members formed a line to congratulate us.

Discussion Questions for A Sinner's Cry!

1. Denise Reese had a Bachelor's in Social Work and a Master's in Business, yet she didn't have a clue that Darren Tate was married. Should she have recognized signs of his deceit?

2. How do you think God feels about folks who only seek Him when they are at their lowest and abandon Him when they feel all is well?

3. Why do you feel Pastor James Davis never dated a member of the church prior to meeting Denise? Do you think that was a good idea?

4. Do you feel Pastor Davis should have resigned and given up his ministry when he became intimate with Denise?

5. Do you believe Denise grew spiritually in the church?

6. What did you think about Denise's relationship with her mother, Betty?

7. Do you know anyone like Sister Clay? How would you have handled her intrusive nature?

8. Do you believe Denise and Pastor Davis were soul mates?

9. Did Denise handle Sarah's alcoholism the right way?

10. Denise and Diana were very close. Should Diana have been more forceful in insisting that Denise leave Darren alone?

11. Do you feel that people who work in the church have a better opportunity to grow spiritually? Denise worked with the teens and young adults of the church. Do you feel the pastor was right in encouraging her to work with the teens? Why do you feel he felt that would be helpful?